L G.

Jessie Grey; Or, the Discipline of Life

A Canadian Tale

L G.

Jessie Grey; Or, the Discipline of Life
A Canadian Tale

ISBN/EAN: 9783337073077

Printed in Europe, USA, Canada, Australia, Japan

Cover: Foto ©Andreas Hilbeck / pixelio.de

More available books at **www.hansebooks.com**

HOME.

" Standing upon the northern shore of the St Lawrence, whose rushing
waters make ceaseless music as they curve in and out among the picturesque
'Thousand Isles,' there are very few who would not be content to call that
white-walled farmhouse—Home."—*Page* 3.

Frontispiece.

Jessie Grey

Or the Discipline of Life

A Canadian Tale

By L. G.

"I've almost grown a portion of this place ;
I seem familiar with each mossy-stone ;
Even the nimble chipmunk passes on,
And looks, but never scolds me."
—Sangster

NEW YORK
THOMAS NELSON & SONS
1871

PREFACE.

DEAR CHILDREN,

I bring my little book to you with the earnest wish that God's blessing may attend it, and abide with you all your lives long!

I love my native land, my western home, very, very dearly; and you, the children of our country, share in this love, and hold strong possession of my heart. For, looking into the future, I see in you, now so young and weak, the power that will move a mighty nation for good or evil.

I believe that it depends, in a very great degree, upon the lessons learned and ideas implanted in your childhood, to make you the strong, earnest men and women our country will need. *First* of all these lessons comes—trust in God.

A man who does not love God *may* love his country; but the true patriot is always the true Christian.

Make this your study, dear children, to know and follow Him who "hath so loved the world." Trusting and serving Him, we need not fear to leave in your hands the care of our beloved country.

He is faithful and true who hath promised to be "strength in the time of trouble to all who put their trust in Him."

For you, more especially, little girls, I have written the following pages ; and if, through them, I help you to realise how uncertain and unstable the strongest earthly support is—if they help you to find the only reliable stronghold, in giving your hearts to the one sure Friend, my object shall have been well accomplished.

An earnest, Christian woman, whether mother,

sister, or daughter, cannot but have a strong influence in leading the home-hearts to things "honest, pure, and of good report," and in this influence lies her peculiar mission and path of duty. By the use of it alone, she fulfils her duty to God and her native land, and does her part in strengthening and purifying the nation ; "If there be any virtue, and if there be any praise, *think on these things.*"

CONTENTS.

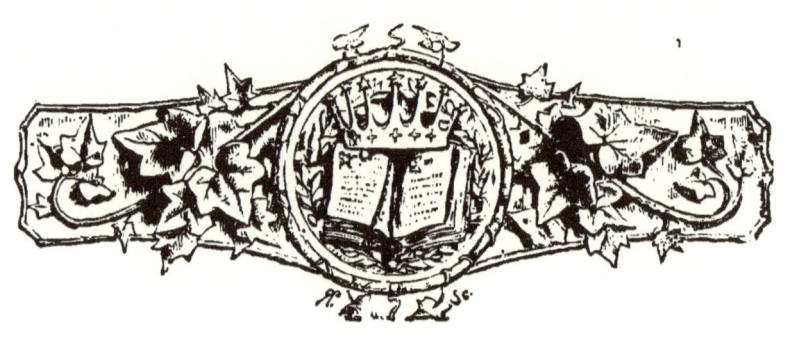

CHAPTER I.

Days of Sunshine.

"O little feet! that such long years
  Must wander on through hopes and fears,
  Must ache and bleed beneath your load;
  I, nearer to the wayside inn
  Where toil shall cease and rest begin,
  Am weary, thinking of your road!"

"MAMMA! mamma! where are you?" sounds the merry voice of Willie Grey, as he runs hastily from one room to another, in his quiet farmhouse home.

"I think she must be down in the milk-cellar," he concludes, after a fruitless search through the house; and hurrying down the path, he finds that he has guessed correctly.

Mrs Grey is in the milk-cellar, busily arranging milk-pans, and working over a great bowl of butter, fresh from the morning's churning. She looks up to the bright eager face of her boy as he stands before the door, with the smile that can come only from a mother's pride and tenderness.

"O mamma! can we go fishing? The boat is all ready, and Jessie and Allie are waiting upon the bank. Do let us, please! We'll bring such splendid fish for supper; and you know school begins to-morrow, so this is our last day."

"But will it not be very warm upon the water so early in the afternoon, Willie? and, you remember, Allie was not very well this morning."

"But we have an umbrella, mamma, and will keep in the shade of the islands as much as possible."

His eager, pleading face shows that his heart is quite fixed on the pleasant sail; and the mother's love cannot resist it.

"Well, you may go, my son; but be very careful; and do not get too far away," she answers, cheerfully.

With a joyful "Thank you, mamma!" and promising to remember her directions, Willie runs hastily for his fishing-lines, bounds quickly through the shaded paths of the garden, and in a very few moments has pushed off the little canoe, in which his sisters are already seated.

Leaving them to enjoy their sail, we will come back and make a longer visit to the pleasant farmhouse. Very quiet and home-like it looks in the afternoon

2

sunshine of this warm August day. Standing upon
the northern shore of the St Lawrence, in one of the
most beautiful regions through which the grand old
river runs, very few persons, I fancy, would find fault
with its situation and surroundings. Built upon a
slight elevation but a few yards back from the river,
whose rushing waters make ceaseless music as they
curve in and out among the picturesque "Thousand
Isles," and wash the gray rocks in front, there are
very few who would not be content to call that white
walled farmhouse—Home.

The interior of the house, with its large, low rooms
and wide fireplaces, its corner cupboards and old-
fashioned furniture, well fulfils the promise of comfort
suggested by its outside appearance.

The milk-house, where we left Mrs Grey, consists of
a single room, built so close to the water's edge that
the smooth stone floor is always damp and cold. A
single rock forms the wall upon one side, and the
other sides and roof are so covered with wild-grape
vines, that a stranger would never suspect that rolls
of golden butter, and rows of well-filled milk-pans, are
kept cool and fresh beneath their shade.

Sit down with me upon the grass-plot under the
wide-spread branches of this American elm, and with
the blue, free waters rolling at our feet, and the loving
atmosphere of home wafted to us from the pleasant

3

house : I will tell you of its inmates, and, as far as I can, relate their histories.

We will go back through the years of our century that are already gone, to eighteen hundred, and stand, in imagination, upon the deck of a vessel just leaving the shores of "Bonnie Scotland" for the far-away Western World. Among the many hopeful ones who are now looking tearfully, "for the last time," at their native land, is a brave Glasgow laddie of twenty years.

Stout-hearted as he is, the courage of Robert Grey almost fails him when the last rope is thrown upon the deck, and the final parting comes. He feels already the home-sick yearning for friendly faces and familiar scenes, and half regrets his decision to leave them all. Toil and danger, perhaps death, await him in the wild country to which he is bound, and a vision of his father's house, and the bustling, active street, for a moment, throws the unknown future into very dark shadow.

But more hopeful thoughts come soon, as he remembers the wide, unexplored lands, the rich, uncultivated soil, which labour and energy will so soon make productive.

Bright dreams of honour and prosperity drive away the present sadness, and, with God's blessing, he resolves to be all that industry and honesty can make him in his adopted land.

4

It is sixty years since that resolution was made. If you ask how it was kept: think of the brave heart that upheld him during a long period of active warfare against the numberless trials and difficulties of a new settlement; the untiring energy that was needed to convert a wilderness into a garden. Look over these broad fields in all their rich productiveness. Speak of him to the many who respected and loved him in life, and who honour his memory now. Stand over his grave, and read how he went triumphantly to the Christian's home, when "old and full of days;"—and these will answer you.

There were many dark days of toil and privation, many hardships to encounter; but trust in God, and the brave heart within him, upheld him through them all. He worked at first in the vicinity of York, now known as Toronto; but, at the close of the war of 1812, settled upon this farm, a few miles from Brockville, one of the most beautifully situated towns in Western Canada.

Ten years ago he died, leaving his only son, the present Robert Grey, to possess the fields he had toiled for, and the good name he had won.

Mrs Grey, who has long ago finished her work in the milk-cellar, and gone to the house, is the grand-daughter of a United Empire loyalist,—one of a class who desired that Britain and America should

5

remain united. The adjoining farm is her happy girlhood's home; and to her, there is no dearer place on earth than this sunny slope on the St Lawrence shore.

But see! the children are coming back from their fishing excursion, and we will go to meet them.

You have already seen bright, twelve-years-old Willie, who carries so proudly the promised string of fish. The larger of the girls is brown-eyed Jessie, two years older than her brother; and the wee golden-haired lassie she holds by the hand, is little Alice, who has just counted her eighth birthday.

The canoe is drawn up high on the sands and fastened securely to the great log, and then, talking earnestly, they walk along the shore, towards the house. But Allie spying "mamma at the door!" the conversation is broken off, and their tongues are soon running busily as they tell of their afternoon's adventures.

Milking-time comes, and Willie, taking the pails, coaxes Allie away with him to "help to milk, while mamma and Jessie get tea ready."

The August sun sets, leaving a bright flush upon the water, and lighting up the islands with new beauty.

The foaming milk-pails have been brought to the house, and the milk strained into the shining row of pans prepared for it. Supper has been eaten—Willie's fish duly praised, and Jessie's busy fingers have helped to wash and set away the dishes.

The family are sitting before the door in the pleasant twilight. Mr Grey, tired with his labour in the harvest-field, is lying upon the wooden seat beneath the window; and the children are grouped about their mother upon the steps.

They are still talking of what they had seen and said in their sail and ramble among the islands.

"We stopped at Chimney Island, mamma," says Willie ; "and Jessie sat there, trying to make herself believe that the old chimney was a great castle, like the ones Sir Walter Scott tells about in his poems, and that we had been driven there by a storm and were just waiting for the warder to admit us."

"And Willie pretended," says Jessie, "that the block-house stood there, strong and new, with the cannons upon the embankment, and that the old magazine was still full of powder and bombs, and he was one of the red-coated soldiers who defended it, while the enemy upon the islands were preparing for the attack."

"And what did my little Allie think of?" asks Mrs Grey.

"Oh, I don't know, mamma. I listened to Jessie and Willie, and liked to hear them talk, and was glad that the cannons and soldiers were not needed on our islands now; but as we sat in the shade of the steep rock, I thought how pleasant it was to get out of the hot sunshine, and a verse that papa read this morning came into my mind, about ' the shadow of a great rock in a weary land,' and I felt how beautiful it was ! "

" Yes," says her mother, " that is the way with us all. If you had not been made uncomfortable first, by the warm sunshine, you would not have realized how cool and refreshing the shade was ; and in the same way we do not feel the love and presence of God until trouble or danger shows us our need of Him."

They are all quiet for a time, and then Jessie begins to sing, softly, the Evening Hymn. Her mother and brother join in the second verse, and when they have finished, and the last echo of their voices has died away from among the trees and islands, Mr Grey arises and talks with them of that happy land, where an everlasting home is prepared for all who love God and do His commandments.

And then they kneel in the open air, while he prays that their heavenly Father will protect and keep them, and bring them, at last, to join those who have crossed the dark river and entered that land, to dwell "for ever with the Lord."

In a few moments, quietness and slumber have settled upon the house, and the blue St Lawrence waters sweep on towards the broad Atlantic just as they swept two hundred years ago, when the wigwam of an Iroquois chieftain stood where its white walls stand.

The noble old river has witnessed many changes and bitter conflicts in the passing of these years. The beautiful hunting-grounds that the Indian then roamed over in unfettered freedom, have passed into the possession of civilised and Christian men; and the white-winged messengers of commerce and peace float where his bark canoe then glided. The wild war-whoop has given place to the shriek of the steam-engine, and the noise of savage battle to the hum of busy machinery. And, better than all else, true Christian hearts are lifted in prayer to a known and only God, instead of blind worship paid to a mystical and dreaded spirit. And with the heritage of this goodly land, are granted to its inhabitants liberties and privileges enjoyed by very few other nations. " The lines are fallen unto *us* in pleasant places ! "

CHAPTER II.

Summer Clouds.

"Faith alone can interpret life, and the
    Heart that aches and bleeds with the stigma
Of pain, alone bears the likeness of Christ,
    And can comprehend its dark enigma."
                    —LONGFELLOW.

ALL the next morning, while Jessie Grey is engaged with her work and studies, the memory of what her mother said the night before, about trouble being necessary to bring the heart to God, is in her mind.

"I wonder what sorrow will come to me, to make me love Him more?" she thinks. "Oh, how I wish I could feel as mamma does about such things!"

Willie and Allie have gone to school, so there is nothing to draw her attention from the few words, fitly spoken, that had attracted it.

10

The children attend the district school, nearly two miles away; but for the last few months Jessie has read and recited with her mother at home. Her parents intend that she shall have the advantage of a course of study in a college or ladies' seminary, but until her tastes and habits are more developed and settled, they think home and home-influences the best teachers. Mrs Grey's education had been a thorough one, and her daughter's attainments are in no danger of standing still under her care.

The warm summer morning wears away, and the long noon rest that Mr Grey allows himself and his harvesters is over.

Jessie brings her books to the pleasant sitting-room, and sits down by her mother's side, prepared to recite her lessons.

Mrs Grey has observed the unusual thoughtfulness of her little daughter several times through the day, and seeing that her mind is now far away from the history lesson she is attempting to read, she asks, playfully, "Can you not decide between King and Parliament, Jessie? or is it some nearer trouble than poor King Charles's?"

"Oh yes, mamma; I've been thinking all day of what you said last night, and I can't understand how trouble and care can make us better. It seems to me that I would love God more if He would let me be always happy, than if I knew and felt that He had sent some great sorrow upon me."

"Who knows best what is for our good, Jessie?"

"God does, of course, mamma."

"And if we believe that He knows what we need, and that He is too merciful and loving to afflict us without cause, can we not take whatever He sends as a proof of His love?—can we not trust that each trial but shows His watchfulness and care over us?"

"But I cannot see, mamma, why He should make us suffer if He loves us so; I 'm sure we do not like to give pain to people we care for."

"When you were a little girl, Jessie, you were sometimes punished for faults that were at the time very trifling, but which, if allowed then, would have grown to be very serious ones. You suffered pain at the time, and perhaps thought your papa and I very cruel; but do you love us less now, or believe that we would have punished you needlessly?"

"Oh no, mamma, because I can understand now that it was for my good, and that it was necessary."

"And just so, my daughter, trials that seem 'too great to be borne,' turn out to be our greatest blessings, and we will, sooner or later, recognize our Father's hand and be strengthened in believing 'that He doeth all things well.' It is not always a sudden or great sorrow that brings us to this belief," continues Mrs

12

Grey; "sometimes it is learned from every-day cares and the little vexations of everyday life."

"Put away your books for this afternoon, Jessie; and I will tell you how the lesson was taught my grandmother."

Histories and grammars are quickly placed upon Jessie's own shelf in the tall bookcase, and she seats herself in the shaded doorway, with her work-basket at her side, to listen to the promised story.

"You have read of the American revolution," says her mother, "and remember how that, in the year 1776, the greater part of the colonists of New England thought themselves justified in breaking off their relations with the mother-country, and setting up a government of their own. My grand-parents had then been married but a short time.

"Grandmother's ancestors were among the first settlers in America, and, at the opening of the war, her father and brothers took sides with the revolutionists, while her husband remained a royalist.

"They were living upon a well-cultivated farm in Massachusetts, and were surrounded by all the comforts and luxuries of an old-settled country. But when the strife became one between principle and self-interest, my grandfather did not hesitate to sacrifice the latter. He had been educated so thoroughly into a love of monarchical institutions, that no inducements could prevail with him to surrender them. All through the six years of the war, those who had been his warmest friends were at enmity with him; and when it was closed, by Great Britain recognising the independence of the States, he was forced to leave his beautiful home and begin life again in a new country.

"As was natural, my grandmother's heart clung very closely to her old home and friends, but she knew it was vain to try to influence her husband in the stand he had taken 'for conscience' sake.' She said good-bye to the fair homestead and household goods that were so dear, and came to Canada with only a half-hearted agreement in the necessity for the sacrifice. She remained at Montreal, while my grandfather came here to prepare a house for the family; and I have often heard her tell of the chilly November evening upon which she arrived at her new home, and the bitter comparisons she made between the little log cabin, and the commodious farm-house she had left for it.

"And when the long Canadian winter set in, her discontent increased every day.

"They had been obliged to leave all but the plainest and most necessary articles of furniture, and even these were crowded in the two tiny rooms their cabin boasted. Instead of the abundant variety of food to which they had been accustomed, they were able to

procure but a limited supply of the commonest neces-
saries. The heart of the thrifty New-England housekeeper sighed, regretfully, for the well-filled pantries
of her old home; or, as my grandfather would say,
jestingly, she 'wept when she remembered the flesh-
pots of Egypt!' It was a great change from the
thickly-settled neighbourhood they had left.

"The small clearing in which the house stood was
completely shut in, on three sides, by naked forest
trees, and the fast-frozen river in front seemed to
separate her from all society, and luxury, and happiness. The winter passed away, and March came with
its boisterous winds and deep snowdrifts.

"With all their privations the family had, as yet,
enjoyed excellent health, but my grandfather came in
one night from the woods, where he had been chopping
all day in the wet, weary and chilled; and the next
morning found him very ill. For many weeks my
grandmother watched and tended him, all other causes
of complaint forgotten, and all other sorrows as nothing
compared with this! Death came very very near her
humble home, and in the shadow of his dread presence,
she felt how ungrateful her murmuring had been, and
acknowledged the justness of its punishment. Strength
and health did not come back to the sick man, until
the first warm days of spring; and in all that time, my
grandmother was without other assistance than that of

a little girl, six years of age, my Aunt Nellie. But repining and regret for the past were ended. Her husband had so nearly approached death, that she realized how comparatively small the loss of other friends was; and real discomforts seemed but trifles, when compared with what might have been.

" She has often said, when talking of those early days in her Canadian home, 'If it had not been for the breaking up of old habits and associations, caused by our removal and the hardships that attended it, it is very likely that I would never have found how insufficient all earthly supports are ; or have felt my need of a higher source of dependence. God saw that my heart was in danger of being filled with the " cares of this world, and the deceitfulness of riches," and took away the causes of them, for a time, that I might remember Him.' And so you will find, my daughter," concludes Mrs Grey, " that all our seeming ills are blessings in disguise, and all our trials are necessary in the discipline of life."

" How glad I am, mamma, that we do not live in those old days, and do not have to go through the hardships and dangers that the early settlers did ! "

" We have great reason to be thankful, Jessie, and to remember with gratitude the brave men who toiled and suffered in securing our homes, who sacrificed their wealth and imperilled their lives, to gain and preserve for us the birthright which we enjoy.

" Canada may well be proud of her founders ; and her sons of the present and future can do no nobler work in guarding and improving her institutions, than their fathers did in laying the foundations and preparing the way for their building. But I have talked long enough, now ; and I am sure you will not forget the moral of my story."

" I will try not, mamma. Thank you for helping me out of my difficulty. I think I understand what puzzled me so ; and yet I can't help wishing that sorrow may stay away from *me*. I have always been so happy, that I can't bear to think of a change."

Her quick, joyous step, as she runs to meet her brother and sister on their way home from school, shows that the passing cloud is all dispelled from her mind.

Very fervently does Mrs Grey pray that the light heart of her child may not be burdened for a long, long time, by the sad experiences that bow down so many of Earth's children.

The road to the school-house winds along the bank of the river for nearly half the distance, and then enters the woods.

Jessie finds Willie and Allie seated upon a great moss-covered rock, which they have named " The Half-

17   C

way House," and where they generally stop to rest, going to and from school.

Allie's basket is almost filled with a varied collection of snail-shells, bits of moss, leaves and flowers, a deserted bird's-nest, and a quantity of winter-green berries; while Willie's satchel is heavy with a fortune of "gold-bearing quartz!" that looks very like mica and iron-pyrites to Jessie's eyes.

They have much to tell of their new teacher and the examination she had made to find how much they already know.

Willie is to begin book-keeping, and, in imagination, he has already taken upon himself the care of the farm accounts, and thereby saved unheard-of sums.

"And I'm to read in the fourth class, and begin to study grammar," says Allie. "Oh! I'm so glad, and I must hurry to tell mamma;" and she jumps from her seat, and dances gleefully along the road, followed by her brother and sister.

Willie is evidently very much in love with his new teacher. "I tell you what, Jessie," he exclaims, "she's just first-rate. The scholars were quieter than I ever knew them to be before, and yet she never spoke loudly, or as though she felt cross, once. *I* intend to like her, and study real hard, any way." His lively imagination flies on from this, through and beyond school-going days, to the use he will make of his education, and the great things he intends to accomplish "when he is a man!"

They soon reach home, where the news must all be told again to "papa" and "mamma," and their sympathy received.

And the sun goes down, and the bright sunset clouds give way to the long summer twilight, from whose mists arises the quiet night. And the calm moon looks down on many happy homes in our fair Canada, but upon none more peaceful and contented than that of Jessie Grey.

HOME.

" A dearer, sweeter spot than all the rest,
　Where man, creation's tyrant, casts aside
　His sword and sceptre, pageantry and pride,
　While in his soften'd looks benignly blend
　The sire, the son, the husband, brother, friend :
　Here woman reigns ; the mother, daughter, wife,
　Strews with fresh flowers the narrow path of life ;
　In the clear heaven of her delightful eye,
　An angel-guard of loves and graces lie ;
　Around her knees domestic duties meet,
　And fireside pleasures gambol at her feet.
　Where shall that land, that spot of earth, be found ?
　Art thou a man ? a patriot ? look around ;
　Oh, thou shalt find, howe'er thy footsteps roam,
　That land thy country, and that spot thy home."
　　　　　　　　　　　　　—MONTGOMERY.

CHAPTER III.

𝔄 𝔇𝔞𝔶 𝔞𝔱 𝔖𝔠𝔥𝔬𝔬𝔩.

" Sweet promptings unto kindest deeds
    Were in her very look ;
  We read her face, as one who reads
    A true and holy book."

—WHITTIER.

I T is Friday morning, the 31st of August,
    and the last day of the summer months.

To-morrow, another season begins—the
season in which trees and plants yield their increase—the golden, fruit-bearing autumn !

We will go with Allie and Willie, this morning, and be first to write our names in the
Visitors' Book of this new term at the district
school.

It is about half-past seven, as we leave the
house, already made neat and orderly for the
day, and start upon our two miles' walk.

A ridge of land rises, close to the water's edge,

a quarter of a mile away, on the top of which Allie stops us, to "take a last look at home."

"Isn't it funny?" says Willie, as we stand upon the high bank and look over the sparkling river; "it seems so strange to think that nearly all this water has come away from Lake Huron, or Superior, or even farther, and has taken that great flying-leap at Niagara on its way."

"Yes," answers Allie; "and think of all the towns, and cities, and houses it has passed in the miles that lie between, and the number of people who have sailed upon it and watched it!"

"How I wish it could tell us all it has seen; don't you, Allie? What a long story it would be! I mean to go away up to Manitoulin Island when I am a man, and sail down from there. I'll take you too, Allie, if you'll go."

"When you are a man—I don't know, Willie—I suppose I would like it, but we can't tell what may happen. Someway," she goes on, musingly, "the river from here always makes me think of that 'pure river of the water of life, clear as crystal,' that it tells about in Revelation. It is so perfectly beautiful! It seems as if there couldn't be a lovelier place in the world."

"*I* don't believe there is," asserts Willie. "But we shall be late for school, if we stay here any longer, and that wouldn't be very nice."

"I don't see how you always remember your Bible verses," he continues, as we walk on ; "I scarcely ever think of them ; but they seem to be in your mind all the time, and one is ready for everything."

"Beautiful things seem to bring them to my mind," answers Allie ; "they say just what I feel, and no other words can."

And now we enter the woods. The shade is very pleasant even at this early hour, and the perfume of ferns and flowers and decaying wood fills the air with fragrance.

Sweet-voiced birds are singing in the overhanging branches of elms, hickories, and maples, and myriad insects are busily getting together their stores of winter food. Here and there a brisk squirrel peeps out from behind a tree-trunk, or scampers from log to log, in well-feigned alarm and anxiety to reach his own snug nest.

If it were always summer in our Canadian woods, one would be almost content to live as the red man has, with no wish for the boasted advantages of cultivation. Here are subjects for study, enough to engross a lifetime, and here are nature's own best text-books.

But we soon come out again to the road, and then a sudden turn brings the school-house in sight.

There it stands, upon one of those abruptly-terminating hills, so often found in this part of the Laurentian chain. The sloping side of the hill, which stretches away westward as far as the eye can reach, has apparently a considerable depth of fertile soil; but the great mass of sandstone, in front of us, seems to have put a final limit to the elevation in this direction.

Perched upon this enormous rock, is the school-house. Its weather-beaten walls are almost the same colour as the lichens with which its huge foundation is overgrown; and the hot rays of the sun beat down upon its roof, as if to punish it for standing in such an unprotected spot, while so many shaded places are near.

It is not quite nine o'clock, and a group of laughing children run to meet Willie and Allie, their noisy greetings stopped only by the ringing of the bell. The new teacher, Miss Mills, stands at the door, and a very intelligent and pleasant-looking lady we think her, as she smilingly checks the boisterous children, in their hurry to be seated.

There are but thirty names upon the register as yet, for only the younger girls and boys can be spared from the farms, until this busy harvesting and berrying season is over.

The work of the school begins, and goes busily on; bright-eyed Willie Grey, with his clear, ready answers, being generally first in his classes, while gentle, little Allie seems to have already gained the love of her teacher.

Recess comes, and is over; and, by and by, it is noon. Pails and baskets are carried to the grove, and there, with many gay speeches and merry peals of laughter, the dinners are eaten. "How nice it would be to have school out here, instead of in that hot, old school-house!" says a roguish little gipsy who is dancing about, with both hands full of bread and butter.

All agree that it would be, and are overjoyed when Miss Mills says, pleasantly—"*I* have been thinking of the plan, and we will try this afternoon how quiet you can be here."

And now the children scatter about in every direction: some to the side of the spring, where their drinking-vessels vary from tin to folded leaves; some to a neighbouring orchard in search of windfalls; the greater part of the boys to play marbles against the school-house rock; while a few quiet ones remain sitting with their teacher, who reads aloud from a book of poems.

The hour is quickly gone, and with one o'clock the novelty of "school out of doors" begins.

The little scholars are as quiet and attentive as can be expected, and half-past three finds the lessons all recited.

A large bunch of wild-flowers had been brought to Miss Mills at noon; and now, taking them up, she teaches the children to know the different parts of the

24

flower, and explains how -it grows and ripens; how the ovules are nourished and defended until their rootlets and branches are able to strive for themselves in the clear air and the fresh earth, and the tiny embryo becomes a large tree or plant. Then she tells them of the wondrous variety in size and beauty that is produced by the colouring and position of the petals, and from that comes to the old lesson—" Consider the lilies !" The sweet voice is very earnest as it speaks of the Hand that forms and cares for the flowers, and of the Love that watches over little children too, to guard them more lovingly than all else, if they will but trust to it.

The double lesson sinks deep in many a childish heart; and in long years to come the sight of these simple wild-flowers will bring to remembrance the loving Father who watches over all His works, and the gentle voice that told them of His love upon this school-house green.

We take the pleasant walk homeward through the rustling woods, and along the river shore, glad and thankful that in our favoured land so many teachers may be found who enter upon their work, feeling the responsibility that rests upon them, and determined to fulfil their mission well.

There can be no more solemn trust confided than that given to a teacher, for, " What ye write on the tablet remains there still ;" and Jesus said, " Take heed that ye despise not one of these little ones, for in heaven their angels do always behold the face of my Father which is in heaven."

" God might have made the earth bring forth
Enough for great and small ;
The oak tree and the cedar tree,
And not a *flower* at all.

" He might have made enough, enough,
For every want of ours;
For medicine, luxury, and food;
And yet have made *no flowers.*

" Then wherefore, wherefore were they made
All dyed in rainbow light,
All fashion'd with supremest grace
Up-springing day and night ?

" Springing in valleys green and low,
And on the mountains high,
And in the secret wilderness
Where no man passeth by?

" Our outward life required them not ;
Then wherefore had they birth ?
To minister delight to man,
And beautify the earth.

" To comfort man and whisper hope
Whene'er his faith grows dim ;
For God who careth for the flowers,
Will *much more* care for him "

HOWITT.

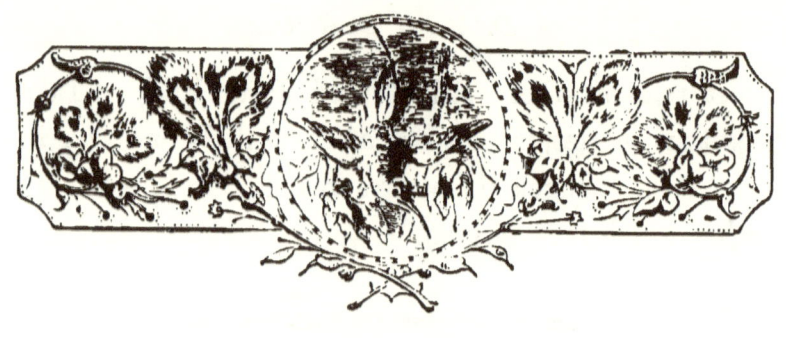

CHAPTER IV.

The "Old Days."

" Not once or twice in our young *nation's* story,
The path of duty was the way to glory :
He, that ever following her commands,—
Shall find the toppling crags of Duty scaled,
Are close upon the shining table-lands
To which our God himself is moon and sun."

ABOUT a mile from Mr Grey's, the river makes a sudden bend that forms a sharp projection of a few acres of land, called The Point.

Upon it stands the old log-house in which his father first settled, and where he was born. It has been inhabited, for the last twenty years, by an old French woman—Madame Bernard—known as "Grandma," or "Granny Bernard," through all the neighbourhood. Though past seventy years old, she still partly supports herself by weaving and knitting for the neighbouring farmers' wives, especially for Mrs Grey.

27

She was born in Lower Canada, and lived there the greater part of her life. She loves dearly to talk of the old days at Quebec, and tell old-time stories of "beautiful France," the far-away land of her fathers. Just as dearly do Willie Grey and his sisters love to listen to these stories, and very few Saturdays pass that they do not visit her.

Come with me through these long, straggling lines of bushes, that, in the times gone by, were trim rows of lilac and currant and gooseberry, that marked the paths of the garden about the old house. The rough logs of which its walls are composed, are all concealed, upon this side, by a luxuriant growth of hop-vines. They have climbed away over the roof, and hang in fragrant clusters over the little porch that shades the doorway in front. Within the porch stands an aged woman, gazing anxiously up the road. The years that have bent the small figure, and silvered the hair, seem to have left undimmed the piercing black eyes, now lighting up with pleasure, as her watching is rewarded by the appearance of the expected guests.

They quicken their steps as they draw near the house, and are soon beneath the pleasant shade of the hop-vines with their old friend.

Willie has brought a basket of cakes, of Jessie's baking, which are to place her among the famous cooks of the age in "Grandma's" estimation, as they already

28

GRANDMA BERNARD.

"The years that have bent the small figure, and silvered the hair, seem to have left undimmed the piercing black eyes, now lighting up with pleasure."—*Page* 28.

have in his own. She welcomes them cheerily, and, with genuine French politeness, provides a glass of cold water and a fan of folded newspaper for each after their long walk.

They are soon rested, and Willie and Allie find a skein of yarn to wind, while Grandma takes her knitting and watches Jessie admiringly as she crimps the border of a new cap sent by her mother.

" And now for a story," says Willie ; " you promised, you know, Grandma, to tell us about the taking of Quebec by the English."

" Ah ! my dear child, that was a sorrowful time for the poor French, though I suppose it is quite right now. Well, you must know, my father came over from his beloved France under the great General Montcalm, when he was sent to aid the colonists of New France against the English in the year 1756. For two years they fought, being successful at Oswego, Fort William-Henry, Carrillon, and Montmorenci ; and then came that day that added Canada to England's empire. General Wolfe, the victorious English leader, began the siege of Quebec in June 1759.

"For nearly three months the army and citizens within held their position ; and then the English, by doing what the French deemed could only be done by a miracle, gained their great advantage. My father has often told us of their wonder and dismay, when they awoke upon the morning of that thirteenth of September, to find the enemy upon the Plains.

"During the night they had landed at the *Fuller's Cove*, surprised the sentries, and climbed the almost perpendicular heights, of nearly three hundred feet, that none but British soldiers would have thought of attempting.

"The French troops were so dispersed, that the part ready to enter the field was very much smaller than the British army; but their beloved Montcalm led them out, and they began the battle. All the world knows the result.

"The British were successful; but young, heroic Wolfe closed his eyes in death upon the victorious field; and brave Montcalm was carried from his last defeat to be buried next morning in the Ursuline Chapel at Quebec.

"My father, a soldier in the ranks, was wounded almost at the same time as his general, and for some days was insensible. When he recovered sufficiently to ask the issue of the battle, the city had been surrendered, and the British had established that power in Canada they have never since lost.

"My mother's ancestors came over from France with Champlain, and had lived in Quebec since its first founding. Her father's house was in the lower town, which had been all destroyed by fire some days before the great battle. They were living in a small, comfort-less room, a little beyond the city, and were in great distress; but they still had sympathy to spare for those who had been wounded in fighting for them. My father was carried from the Plains to their humble dwelling; and for a long time they nursed the poor young soldier, who was suffering so far from his native land. It was many months before he was quite well, and then gratitude and love for the ones who had been so kind to him were stronger than the old home-ties, and he returned to France no more. He was too ill to join the French in their final attempt to regain their possessions; and when the English government was settled, and the people reconciled to the change, he soon secured a comfortable home in the new British colony. My father would often walk over the old battle-ground, while he described to us children how the armies were placed, and upon what spot his general fell. Then he would talk of his bright, handsome face and flashing eye, so well known and loved by all the French soldiers, and tell us of the strange foreboding of ill-fortune that took possession of the brave heart; how a shadow of final overthrow went with him through victory and defeat, that at last affected his soldiers too. 'It was doubtless caused,' my father said, 'by the difficulties they encountered, and by the cruel hunger from which both colonists and soldiers sometimes

31

suffered, through failures in the harvests, and delays in their supplies from France.'"

"And you have seen Wolfe's monument, haven't you, Grandma?" breaks in Willie; "the gallant, glorious Wolfe! who 'died content' when he knew that the British were victorious!"

"Yes, my dear child, very many times; and I am quite as glad as you that he was victorious, though perhaps not quite as proud of him."

"Why are you glad, Grandma?" asks Allie.

"Because that through the coming of the English very many have learned to trust for pardon only in the one precious Sacrifice that was offered for all, instead of in unavailing gifts and penances of their own. Because, I humbly believe, that I myself have been taught by them to find the peace that no earthly absolution can give."

There is a depth and fervency in the voice that utters this simple confession of faith, that leaves no doubt of its earnestness and sincerity.

We cannot give the broken accents and many idioms by which Grandma expresses herself, and which render her narratives all the more charming in the opinions of the children; but this is the substance of her story.

Mr Grey promised to come down in the canoe to take them home, so they are in no hurry to leave their old friend.

32

They have tea, and Jessie's cakes are praised, quite to Willie's satisfaction; and then they sit before the door and sing, while the twilight shadows are lengthening towards the night.

Very sweet do their childish voices sound to the old woman, who is so near the end of her life-journey, as they sing the praises of the only Friend left to her old age. Parents, brothers, children, have all passed; and now, as she draws near the last of her fourscore years, there is no earthly arm upon which she may lean—there is no one left her but her God! The hymns of the children seem to bring His all-sufficient love and presence very near, and her heart rejoices in remembering that His care can never be removed.

Their father comes at last, and with many a kind good-bye, and promise to come again soon, they step into the canoe, and leave the happy old woman in her solitary home.

As they round the point, and come directly opposite the old house, the moon rises, and her bright light shining through from one window to another, for a moment, makes it appear, as Willie exclaims it is, " all afire inside ! "

" I remember a great alarm we had many years ago, owing to those very windows," says his father. " One dark, rainy night, one of my sisters observed a strange light a short distance from the house, and after watching it for some time, spoke to the others about it. It appeared to be of a pale blue colour, and seemed to glide from one place to another, in a ghastly kind of movement. I could not at all account for it. My father spoke of decaying wood, and the *ignis fatuus;* but when, next day, the exact spot was examined and found to be a smooth grass-plot, that of course had to be given up. Our servant-girl, and several of the neighbours who believed in the supernatural, told grave stories of buried gold that had been dishonestly gained, and whispered of unquiet spirits who could not rest until their bodies have been given Christian burial. The children were terribly frightened, and nothing could induce them to approach the mysterious spot. My mother and I, however, started to examine it, but to our surprise, when we had got within a certain distance, the light would disappear. We could see it plainly until we had passed a certain point, and then it was gone. Our report strengthened the belief of the lovers of the supernatural, who told yet more thrilling stories of mysterious lights, to the added terror of the younger ones.

"But my father had noticed that when the windows were darkened, by many persons standing before them, or from any other cause, the light always disappeared.

"You know where the lighthouse stands, a few miles below the point, and how plainly its light can be seen from the old house? Well, by hanging heavy curtains to the windows, upon which the rays from it fell, the spectral light beyond was made to vanish entirely; and my father explained how, by the reflection of the rays from the surface of the water, and through the windows, the false light that had so alarmed us was produced, and that its apparent movement from place to place was caused by the rippling of the water. And so the mystery turned out to be no mystery at all, but only a few harmless rays from the distant lighthouse, falling upon and shining through the panes of glass in our windows.

"All such appearances and apparent mysteries, if properly examined, would be found to proceed from some such cause," concludes Mr Grey; "and a great many of the fearful tales of spectres and ghosts, so often foolishly repeated and believed in, arise from equally simple and harmless incidents." As he finishes speaking, the canoe grates upon the stones at their own landing, and the children spring ashore, resolving never to be very much frightened by a ghost-story, until they have well examined the cause of fear.

CHAPTER V.

An Angel's Visit.

"There is a Reaper, whose name is Death,
     And with his sickle keen,
He reaps the bearded grain at a breath,
     And the flowers that grow between."
                              —LONGFELLOW.

TIME passes quickly and quietly away, making very little change in the happy home-life at the Greys'. The autumn frost has touched with his icy wand the leaves of trees and shrubs, and we find them dressed in more gorgeous robes than when last we saw them.

If possible, the shores and islands that confine and adorn the noble old river are lovelier than before, but there is no change in it ; its waters still hurry with the same resistless power—on to their burial in the great ocean !

It is almost the last of October. The road

to school is strewn with fallen leaves, and many of the birds have left their summer haunts to seek for others far away.

The days are shortening, so that sunset comes very soon after the children get home from school now, and all things speak of the swift passing away of the year.

It is a bright and pleasant afternoon, though the ground is still wet from a heavy shower of rain that fell in the morning.

Jessie is beginning to watch for her brother and sister, and they are just within sight of the house; having reached the high bank that commands Allie's favourite view of the river.

Her hand clasps her brother's, and they are talking too earnestly to notice how near the edge of the dangerous height they are walking.

Ah! why is it that no pitying spirit warns Willie Grey of the sorrow so near him? Why is he allowed to go on so gaily making plans, that the next moment will render less than useless for ever?

The sound of their voices and footsteps startles one of the small green and black snakes, so commonly found near a river, and it rustles out from a bed of leaves, at their very feet.

With a quick, frightened cry, Allie lets go her grasp of Willie's hand, and springs back upon the wet, slippery bank; back so near to the treacherous edge, that she loses her balance, and falls over; and the deep, black waters close over her, almost before her brother knows what has happened.

His first wild impulse is, to plunge after her; but a thought of his insufficient strength, and the great depth of the water there, restrains him. Waving his arms, he screams loudly to his father and two men, who are working in a field at a short distance; and they, with a quick comprehension of his meaning, run hurriedly towards him.

He has seized a long piece of board that was lying near, and is holding it down over the water, that she may grasp it when she rises. But the smooth surface remains unbroken; and the little form he watches for does not appear. His father has come, and has thrown himself into the water, ready to snatch his darling from its cruel depths; but there is still no movement, it is all undisturbed by the uplifted arms and pleading face, so agonisingly looked for!

The canoe is brought up by the men, and he sees them join his father, who is searching for his child, with despairing energy, now!

A terrible fear is settling down upon his heart, that he vainly tries to drive away; a fear that she is drowned; that his little sister is gone from him for ever! Thought and consciousness give way before it at last, and the dread weight of anxiety deadens every sense and feeling.

Some one leads him away, and he awakens to find himself in the house, with Jessie and his mother ; and is wondering what it is that has so changed them all ; that makes everything so dark and sorrowful ?

Then hope is all gone, and the long suspense gives way to despair ; to the dread certainty that their darling is *dead !*

It is nearly an hour before she is found. She had sunk into one of the deep fissures of the river's bed, and her dress catching upon a sharp projecting rock, had prevented her rising.

And she is *dead !* The gentle, loving child, whose voice sounded joyously, an hour ago, as she stood where pitying men now stand and whisper of her death.

She is *dead !* And who will comfort the mother's heart ? Who will soften the father's grief, and turn to blessing this first great burden of sorrow, that has fallen upon the brother and sister, who so loved and cherished her ?

She is *dead !* And they bear the motionless little figure within the saddened home, that only this morning she left so gaily.

Ah ! there are few households that cannot remember such sorrows; there are few parents who have not endured such bereavements. " Our great humanity " is bound together, through sharing in common the suffering of such afflictions ; and almost every heart can look back to some hour of utter hopelessness, when it was unable to remember anything but the dead !

We thank God, and are glad to know that there is a Voice that can penetrate even this hopelessness—that can bring relief to every human heart, however "heavy laden."

The true Christian minds of Mr and Mrs Grey are not long comfortless. They hear their Father whispering tender words of unfailing love ; and bowing before Him, they repeat from their hearts, that old, old assurance of unshaken faith: "The Lord gave, and the Lord hath taken away ; blessed be the name of the Lord."

For a time Willie is completely overcome by sorrow, and cannot be reconciled to his sister's loss. But as his mother talks to him of the brightness of that better country, where they believe their darling is ; and of the loving Saviour, through whom they shall go to her; his hopeful, buoyant nature casts off a part of the present bitterness, in looking forward to that glad meeting. "I will try to be submissive, mamma," he exclaims. "I will try to think that she is waiting for me there; instead of only remembering that she is gone from me here. But, oh ! it seems *so* long, and I will miss her so all the way!" And heavy sobs burst out again from the troubled, boyish heart.

We find poor Jessie in her own room, where she has been ever since her little sister was found. In the struggle that is going on in her heart, there is more than grief to battle with. The flood-gates of sorrow seem to have all opened at once upon the gentle girl; and when she tries to pray for strength and comfort, so many rebellious thoughts darken the way, that she says despairingly, she "cannot find Christ; that she cannot love Him now, and will never, never be happy again!"

Ah! little Jessie, they who would find Christ must be willing to accept the Father's chastening; and the heart must say: "Thy will be done," before the promised Comforter is sent.

May God grant you patience to learn well this great lesson of the Christian's faith; and may your weary child-heart come to Him and find rest!

The long night passes away; and the morning light shines brightly upon the glancing river, and the saddened home upon its banks, where the angel of death has been. It shines in upon a little, white-robed figure that lies strangely still, where kind hands have placed it; in stillness, never to be broken, for the spirit that animated Allie Grey is with the angels now.

The look of perfect peace, that death always leaves upon the features of little children, has settled upon the sweet face, and when Jessie, who is kneeling beside it, lifts her head to look at it, one would think some of that peace had been imparted to her. Her pale face is very sad; but passion and rebellion are all gone, and in its subdued expression is written submission to God's will.

The loving arm that is "stronger than death" supports her; and, in trusting faith, she has cast the burden of her care upon that outstretched arm.

Pitying friends move softly about, speaking of the goodness of the departed child ; and making the necessary preparations for the solemn ceremonies that attend the final parting of the living from the dead.

The school-children come with their teacher, to look for the last time upon the quiet face of their gentle playmate ; and many sad tears express their love for her, and their sorrow that she is gone.

By and by the day comes, when the little coffin, that contains all that is left to them of their darling, is carried out for ever from the home she had so loved.

They lay her in the quiet country graveyard, where her grand-parents rest from their long years of labour ; and the old minister repeats, over the tiny grave, the beautiful words of Scripture promise, beginning : "I am the resurrection and the life, saith the Lord." They sink like healing dew into the hearts of the mourners, filling them with holy thoughts of the One who entered the tomb to consecrate, for all time, its gloomy portals with the remembrance of His presence.

They "hear a voice from heaven saying, Blessed are the dead which die in the Lord," as they turn away from the little grave ; and remember with solemn thankfulness, the blessedness of the loved one they have lost.

And they come away and leave her there ; the little child-flower, of whom the " Lord had need," beside the " bearded grain " of age !

"And their works do follow them." Happy for all who rest in that enclosure, if the influences of their years lead as surely to well-doing, as the few short days of life that were granted to Alice Grey.

CHAPTER VI.

In the Firelight.

WE come back to the lonely farmhouse, so changed from the bright, cheerful place we have known. A strange hush rests within its walls, and upon the home-group, so suddenly and sadly lessened.

They have "buried their dead;" the little form they miss is gone from them for ever; the sweet child-voice they long for is singing in a far-away land, and will never be heard in earthly music again. They have accepted the affliction as from the hand of God, and have acknowledged His right to do as seemeth Him good; but their loving hearts feel deeply the absence of the lost one,

44

and the yearning sense of "something gone that should be nigh," is ever present with them.

The walk to school is a very sad one for poor Willie now. Allie is associated with every object on the way, and memory recalls all their old conversations; and the countless golden plans that will never be realized, that seemed so full of hope and joyousness, as they talked them over upon this path.

For many days there is a sorrowful shade upon the boy's face, and a more thoughtful look comes into the dark eyes, that were always so glad and full of merriment before.

He does not forget his resolve, to try to be ready to meet his little sister; and the thought of her waiting for him, is a strong help in keeping from temptation.

Jessie generally comes to meet him where the path enters the woods; and, sitting upon the great rock that has been danced over so joyously by the little feet of their dead sister, they talk of her happiness, and their own loneliness, and try to comfort one another.

Mr Grey misses drearily the glad embrace and sweet voice that used to welcome him, and brighten his tired evening hours. He sighs as he remembers that they will greet him no more, until the long day of life is over—until the night shadows of *death* have finished all his labours !

But the mother's tender heart feels most deeply the loss of her baby-girl.

The quick, active minds of Jessie and Willie may be engaged and interested in other things; and other matters may for a time make the father forget; but the aching void in her heart is never filled, and its mourning for the dead " will not be comforted."

The loving face is growing very pale and thin, and the quiet step is growing weaker every day; for the heart of the mother is bound very closely to her child, and the silver cord may not be too suddenly broken.

The chilly November winds have snatched the last leaves from the trees, and whirled them about at their will; and old winter is beginning his reign, by scattering his first snow-flakes over the frozen earth.

The wide fireplace, in the pleasant sitting-room we love so well, has long ago been opened; and great, glowing logs burn merrily within it; their flames sending warmth and light through all the room. It seems even more pleasant this cold winter evening, than in its summer airiness; for a cozy, home feeling springs from the very back-log in the huge chimney, and diffuses itself in every ray of light and heat.

Mrs Grey is lying upon a sofa just opposite the fire, and Jessie is nestled down upon the hearth-stone, at her father's feet, looking into the fire, while she sings softly to herself. Willie stands at the window watching the fast falling snow, and thinking sorrowfully of the little grave that it falls upon for the first time.

There is no sound in the room but the crackling of the fire; and the low, half-audible chanting upon the hearth.

"Sing something aloud, Jessie," says her mother, "sing *The Land o' the Leal.* I have not heard it for a long, long time."

Mr Grey's face is buried in his hands as the clear, child-like tones rise in the sweet air and words of the old ballad:

"I'm wearin' awa', Jean, Like snaw-wreaths in thaw, Jean;
    I'm wearin' awa', To the land o' the leal.
There's nae sorrow there Jean, There's neither cauld nor care, Jean,
    The day is aye fair, In the land o' the leal.

"Ye've been leal and true, Jean, Your task is ended now, Jean,
    And I'll welcome you, To the land o' the leal.
Our bonnie bairn's there, Jean, She was baith guid and fair, Jean,
    But, ah! we grudged her sair, To the land o' the leal.

"Sorrow sel' wears past, Jean, And joy is comin' fast, Jean,
    Joy that's aye to last, In the land o' the leal.
Then dry that glistnin' e'e, Jean, My soul langs to be free, Jean,
    And angels wait on me, To the land o' the leal.

"A' our friends are gane, Jean, We've lang been left alane, Jean,
    We'll a' meet again, In the land o' the leal.
Now, fare ye weel, my ain Jean, This world's care is vain, Jean,
    We'll meet and aye be fair, In the land o' the leal."

Her voice falters a little at the second verse, and Willie, breaking away from his sad thoughts at the window, comes to his mother's side, and hiding his face upon her pillow, sobs long and bitterly. She tries vainly to soothe the passionate outburst; the sorrowful mind-picturing in the snow has heaped up such a heavy burden of grief, that it cannot be easily quieted or dispelled.

Jessie leaves the fire when she has finished her song, and comes to the side of her brother; keeping back the tears, that strong sympathy with his feelings has brought to her eyes. She whispers to him that " Mamma's head has been very bad to-day," and with a great effort, the poor boy restrains the sobs that still rise from his full heart, and rests quietly within the loving arms that would so willingly shield him from all sorrow and evil.

Ah! little Willie, come while you may to that comforting presence; cling very closely to that loving bosom; for a darker shadow is gathering over your home, and the light of your mother's love is quickly passing away from you for ever.

Jessie still remains with her mother, after her papa and Willie have gone to bed.

Her thoughtfulness has very much increased, since that bitter conflict with self upon the night of Allie's death; and she has been a great comfort to them all, in the lonely days since then.

The beginning of the new year had been fixed upon as the time for her starting away to school; but as it draws near, and her mother's strength does not return, she has made up her mind to propose that it may be put off for some months.

There have been some severe battles with selfishness before this decision was arrived at, for very few girls of fifteen have stronger love for books and learning than Jessie Grey. But love for her mother, and an earnest desire to do right, are stronger than all else, and the bright visions of school-life are resolutely driven away.

She tells her mother what she has thought, as they sit together before the fire. " You know, mamma, I can keep on with my studies at home, and a few months will not make very much difference. And then the summer will be so much less lonely for you, and you will be quite well by that time."

Mrs Grey's face is pressed closely upon the pillows, and for some moments she does not reply to the loving suggestion of her daughter.

When she speaks at last, Jessie wonders to find that she has been crying, and that something is still deeply agitating her. "What is it, mamma?" she exclaims; "do you think it better that I should go? or has all this talking to-night made you feel worse?"

Mrs Grey draws the slight form of her daughter very close to her, as she asks, in a low, broken voice, " Have

G

you ever thought, Jessie, that I may not get better? that strength and health may never come back to me?"

A convulsive shudder and a bewildered look of surprise and terror are the only answers; and the low voice goes on, "You have been a great comfort to me, my little daughter, through all these weary, sorrowful days; the sight and knowledge of your new-found trust and confidence in God have helped very much to strengthen mine. I hope your faith in Him would not fail you, if He should see fit to take me from you—that you would love and believe in Him still!"

With a smothered cry of agony, Jessie throws herself despairingly upon the sofa, as if she would never wish to rise again.

She does not listen to her mother's voice, as she attempts to comfort her. All light, and goodness, and beauty seem to be shut out from her heart by the sorrowful weight that is bearing her to the earth, and there is nothing left but a dumb sense of pain.

The *possibility* of such a thing has never presented itself; she cannot think of it as possible now. It is too dreadful to be true! She thought she had tasted the very dregs of sorrow when Allie died; but to be deprived of her *mother!* to look forward to a future without her, to live without the love and help and guidance that have never failed her! Oh! she cannot, cannot be reconciled to it!

"My daughter! my little Jessie! try to remember that it is only for a very little time; try to think that I am only going home to my Father's house a little before you. Leave the rest with God; He will care for you, and bring you, too, when your work is done. Oh, my child! may His love strengthen you! May He more than supply my place to you!"

The tender voice is very faint, and a quick reproach touches the heart of the sorrow-stricken girl. She rises instantly, and summoning all her self-command, controls the torrent of passion with which her heart is filled, and assists her mother to prepare for bed.

"Go to God with your trouble, my darling! Do not try to bear it alone, but leave it all with Him," whispers her mother, as she kisses her good-night.

Jessie's heart is almost broken as she goes up to the little room which she and Allie used to share—where they were happy children together a few short months ago! Joyousness and childhood are gone now, and time is touching very heavily the heart that was so light and careless.

She opens the Bible, which she has so often read with her little sister, at one of their favourite chapters, and tries to receive the proffered comfort from its holy words.

But memories of the past, and the sad burden of the present, are too strong; she cannot see for the blinding tears, that will not be kept back ; and leaning her head upon the table, with the book clasped tightly in her hands, she gives way to a fit of weeping that is utterly hopeless and despairing.

It is quieted at last, and lifting her head, she unclasps the Bible again. It opens at the twenty-fifth chapter of Isaiah, and a faint pencil-mark drawn around the eighth verse catches her eye : " He will swallow up death in victory ; and the Lord God will wipe away tears from off all faces ; and the rebuke of His people shall He take away from off all the earth : *for the Lord hath spoken it.*"

She reads the precious promise over and over again, the words sinking down into her heart, calming and soothing the passionate pain she thought nothing could ever quiet again.

Ah ! the same God who inspired the triumphant words of the old prophet so many centuries ago, put it into the heart of the little child to mark them ! And the tiny hands, folded over the peaceful breast, in the distant graveyard, are, through them, pointing her sister upwards to the glorious home and the loving Father who " hath spoken " them.

They call back faith and trust to Jessie's sorely-tried heart, and she goes to sleep repeating them, in confident assurance that He who hath promised to "wipe away tears from off all faces" will care for and strengthen her.

CHAPTER VII.

The Happy New-Year.

"Friends, friends!—oh! shall we meet
In a land of purer day,
Where lovely things and sweet
Pass not away?"
—Mrs Hemans.

THE winter days glide swiftly away, and the anniversary of the one that proclaimed "good-will toward men" casts its mantle of peace over the earth.

There are no "Merry Christmas" greetings interchanged to-day by the quiet household at Mr Grey's. They hear the glad song of the angels, and receive thankfully in their hearts the message of peace; but the dearest of their number is too near the borders of the spirit-land— the surging of the river that lies between strikes too heavily upon their ears—for thoughts of merriment.

53

No severe pain indicates the approach of the dread visitant ; there is no suffering to contend with or alleviate ; there is *nothing to be done !*

Day by day Mrs Grey's strength grows less, and the bright hectic spot deepens upon the wasted cheek ; day by day the loving watchers feel that she is farther from their keeping—that earth is loosening its hold, and death is drawing nearer.

Grandma Bernard has been sent for, and remains at the farmhouse all the time, and one of Mrs Grey's sisters is often with them, so that Jessie has very few opportunities for talking alone with her mother.

The poor girl feels as if she were in a troubled, sorrowful dream, from which something must, by and by, awaken and relieve her. She has not given way to a passionate expression of grief since the night when the prospect of this great woe had first dawned upon her ; it seems to have settled too deep for expression of any kind, and her face wears a look of despondency that it is very sad to see upon one so young.

The verse that quieted her that night is ever in her mind : "The Lord will wipe away tears from off all faces; the Lord hath spoken it." "She cannot go against His word," she repeats to herself again and again ; "she must not weep when He has said He would wipe away all tears."

But it is a forced yielding to a necessity, not the

cheerful submission God requires. She sees no love in the Hand that strikes the blow, and accepts it only because it *must be*—because there is no alternative— while her heart rises in bitter rebellion.

Willie has been told, but he will not believe; he declares that it is all a mistake, and that his mother will be well again. "Why, Jessie, we could not do without her!" he exclaims; "God knows how much we need her, and He will not take her from us!"

And he persists in this belief, and will not be persuaded from it. Every day he hopes to find her better, and still drives away the fear that it may be possible after all.

The Christmas-week passes away, and the last day of the old year draws near its close.

A bed has been moved into the large sitting-room, because of it size and cheerfulness; and here we find Jessie sitting beside her mother.

The last rays of the sun shine in through the western windows, and brighten the room with almost summer radiance.

Mrs Grey watches the last bright lines sink beneath the wintry horizon, and then, turning to her daughter, she repeats a part of the glorious vision that was granted to one of God's faithful servants, and by which many of His children have expressed their foresight of the heavenly city: "And there shall be no night there;

and they need no candle, neither light of the sun, for the Lord God giveth them light ; and they shall reign for ever and ever."

"My little Jessie ! this will comfort you when I am gone. Remember how happy I shall be. I 'shall see His face.' I shall be with Him to whom you pray— for ever at rest ! You will miss your mother drearily, my child ; but let that draw you still nearer to the God in whom she trusted. I would willingly stay with you ; I would that my love might shield and direct you ; but I know that ' what He wills is best,' and can trust it all to Him."

The long restraint that Jessie has placed upon her feelings gives way, and with a despairing—" Oh ! mamma, mamma ! I cannot let you go ! " the unnatural calmness is broken up.

She feels now that it has not been submission to God, or trust in Him, that has upheld her ; but only a determined resistance to sorrow, which she has built upon the frequent repetition of that Scripture passage. Instead of saying, " Not my will, but Thine, be done ! " she has only recognized the impossibility of the bitter cup being removed from her, with no conviction of the infinite Love and Wisdom that prepared it.

"God has seemed so far away from me, mamma," she says, " I have felt as if I were shut out from His

56

presence; and when I tried to pray, I could only remember that He was taking you from me."

"My poor child! why have you not told me all this before? I thought, from your quiet face, that you had found peace in entire resignation to God's will; and was glad that you had been enabled to leave it all with Him."

"And I fancied, too, mamma, that I was resigned; but I have been so unhappy—I have not felt at all as you do about it."

" 'He that loveth father or mother more than Me is not worthy of Me,'" repeats Mrs Grey. "Have you kept Him *first* in your heart, Jessie? Have you remembered the unbounded love, so much beyond *mine*, that He feels for you—the love that has supplied all the good gifts of your life—that has kept me with you all these years, and is now ready to supply *all* your need? There is nothing to be sorry for on my account. 'I *know* in whom I have believed,' and am glad to hear His voice calling me home! My own little Jessie! He who has been my strength will be yours. Can *you* not trust Him, and give yourself unreservedly to His keeping?"

There is silence in the darkening room for a few moments; but the ear of the Omnipresent Father hears the lowest cry of all who plead, through the merits of His Son; and He is "very pitiful" to His sorrowing children on earth.

A voice whispers peace to the troubled, girlish heart, and doubt and fearfulness are dispelled.

"I *do* believe that He will care for me, mamma, and will no longer grieve Him by selfish murmurings. I do say 'Thy will be done,' and trust in Him altogether."

Jessie's voice expresses a confident determination and strength of purpose, that are new to its quiet tones—a confidence that can manifest itself only when the love of God is felt in the heart.

Ah! what would become of the innumerable hearts that are every day made "heavy laden" by earth's sorrows, if it were not for this "all-sufficient" Love? Well for suffering humanity that there is something more enduring than the strongest earthly refuge, that there are everlasting arms beneath the protecting ones that pass away, that death is powerless to remove.

Trusting in the strength of the crowned Conqueror of the king of terrors, Jessie Grey feels that she is able to bear even the loss of her mother's love.

Tender, regretful thoughts come as often as before, and many sad tears are shed as the first days of the new year pass away; but it is sorrow sanctified by submission, and not "without hope."

Nearly three weeks are gone since, in that quiet

evening-hour, Jessie unburdened her heart of its weary load, and, guided by her mother's hand, found the peace that is given to those who earnestly and prayerfully come to God for help and deliverance.

It is the 19th of January. For several days Mrs Grey's strength has lessened very rapidly, and now the sad, unmistakable look that always comes over the features as the end draws near is written very plainly upon the sweet face.

No fear or doubt troubles her mind as she approaches "the valley of the shadow of death" He to whom her life's work has been given, and in whose name alone she has trusted, is with His children "even unto the end;" and she will not now distrust the strength upon which she has relied for so many years.

Life is fast retreating from the weakened frame, and all day long there is the sound of hushed weeping in the house, as friends and neighbours sorrowfully recognise how close to the limits of that "other life" their loved one has already passed. The hours of daylight wear away, and, as the evening closes, consciousness awakens, and in part drives away the heavy torpor that weakness has imposed.

Jessie and Willie are standing together beside her when she first rouses herself; and as her eyes rest upon them, the tender ineffable light of a mother's love shines in their depths.

"I will be with you but a very little time, my children," she says, quietly. "My Father has sent His messenger to me, and I gladly obey the summons. The sting of death has been taken away, and I go to Him without a fear, knowing that 'to die is gain,' for them who die in the Lord! I expect to meet you there by and by, when you have finished your course. I believe that you will be enabled to keep the faith— that you will strive earnestly to follow Him in whom alone is fulness of joy. Never be turned aside from this ; never let anything stand between you and His love, and He will keep you from the evil of the world, and bring you to share in His glory."

It is only by painful effort, and many long pauses to gain strength, that she has been able to speak these words ; and her eyes close wearily again as voice and memory fail, and sleep overpowers the exhausted faculties.

There is no sound in the room but the sobs of Willie, and Jessie's more silent crying, until Mr Grey comes round from the foot of the bed, and gently drawing his boy within his arms, tries, by whispered words of comfort to quiet his piteous weeping.

For long hours they watch the pure, white face; thinking, many times, that the gentle breathing has ceased altogether, until again, by some slight movement, life asserts its presence.

It is after midnight, and Willie, completely tired out, is sleeping in his father's arms, when, in the last struggle with death, mind and reason for a short time resume their sway.

Grandma Bernard and Jessie have been chafing the cold limbs, wrapping warm flannels about them, and using all those despairing means by which we try to keep the passing spirit a little longer in its earthly home. She feels how hopeless her labour is ; but she cannot bear the chill that is creeping over her mother's frame—that mother who has guarded and protected her from every cold breath all her life long ! She cannot bear to think that that mother is powerless in the cold embrace of death !

Mrs Grey opens her eyes, and smiles with perfect consciousness upon her daughter ; and then, drawing the sad, pale face close to her own, in a clear voice she implores a blessing from on high to rest upon and attend her child. "Keep her from evil, oh ! my Father ! Lead her in straight paths, and be Thou her shield in every time of trouble, until her life-journey is finished and immortality is gained," is the prayer that is spoken over the bowed head of the weeping girl. "And now good-bye, my daughter ! Kiss me good-bye for the last time, until

I greet you in the land that is free from all care and sorrow."

Jessie's lips are pressed again and again upon the sweet face, from which death itself cannot remove the seal of a mother's love; and then she moves quietly away, in obedience to her father's touch, that Willie may take her place.

A solemn look of awe and inexpressible grief has taken the place of the childish sorrow, with which he had before approached his mother. She clasps him in her arms, brushing back the clustering hair from the fair brow with the old tender caress he will never know again. "Promise me, my boy, that you will meet me in heaven; that you will, all your life, strive earnestly for the home prepared for you by a Saviour's love!"

There is no hesitation in either the face or voice that answers, quietly, " I promise you, mamma ! I promise you, by the help of God!" Something of the more than earthly strength by which his mother is supported seems to have been imparted to the boy's nature, generally so impulsive and free from all restraint.

He stops to kiss once more the white lips, parted by shortening breath, and then joins his sister upon the other side of the bed, while Mr Grey bends over to listen to the last low tones of the voice that has made music in his home for so many years.

She repeats her assurance that "all is well," both for her and them, and whispers her gratitude that the passage of the dark river has been made so easy to her feet.

And then a smile that no *earthly* joy could waken brightens the pure face—a smile that does not altogether fade away when the spirit has passed to the full realization of that happiness whose glorious dawning animated it.

The first faint beams of morning light are heralding the birth of another day, as the knowledge comes to Jessie and Willie Grey that all that speaks of life in the mortal frame has for ever departed from the motionless form before them—the sad, sad knowledge that they are *motherless !*

Jessie—remembering a charge given in one of the last conversations with her, that she must try to supply her loss to her papa and Willie, and, as far as possible, fill the place that she was leaving—leads her brother to her own, quiet little room, where, weary with the long night-watching, his sorrow is soon forgotten in the dreamless sleep of boyhood.

Finding that her papa is lying down in his own room, she obeys the advice of many kind voices, that bid her try to get some rest and sleep herself. Poor child ! her pale, patient face looks as if she sadly needed them both !

We need not recount the events of the next few days ;—the coming and going of sympathising friends ; the performing of the last sad offices to the dead ; the watching beside the shrouded figure, that seems less a part of the one we have loved in life, than a shadowy image, bearing a partial and undefined resemblance to the lost ; the strange mingling of bustle and quiet ; and, at last, the closing of the coffin-lid upon what has been a mother's face, and the resigning of all that it contains to the frozen snow-covered earth.

Ah ! if it were not for the hope of immortality—if it were not for the Sun of Righteousness, that shines through and over the cypress trees we plant about their graves—what would sustain us in these trials ? what would comfort us for the loss of our departed friends ?

" But thanks be to God, which giveth us the victory, through our Lord Jesus Christ ! "

CHAPTER VIII.

Going Away.

" I know thy burden, child. I shaped it. . . .
    For even as I laid it on, I said,
    I shall be near, and while she leans on me
    This burden shall be mine, not hers :
    So shall I keep my child within the circling arms
    Of my own love."

HE winter snow has lain heavily upon the
new-made graves in the old burying-
ground upon the St Lawrence shore, and
the blustering March wind is beginning to
drift it from hill-tops and unprotected plains to
sheltered nooks beyond its farther reach, when
we again visit the home of Jessie Grey.

Their old French friend is still with them,
and a Western cousin of Jessie's, but a few years
older than she is, has been a visitor for several
weeks.   But there is a vacancy that *no* other can
fill, and though time has somewhat accustomed
them to their loss, they feel it as keenly as at first.

All thought of self and selfish sorrow seems to have been banished from Jessie's mind, and she has kept far better than she has any idea of the sacred charge given by her mother to supply her place.

The discipline of suffering through which she has passed is yielding plentiful fruit in that "patient continuance in well-doing," which is the best attribute and ornament of true womanly character.

Only God is witness of the conflict that is never quieted between the yearning, loving heart of the child, and the faithful discharge of daily duties. Only His grace could enable her to maintain that apparent calmness, and even cheerfulness, which so effectually covers the never-forgotten *want*, that only a motherless girl can feel.

Information has been received from Mr Grey's relatives in Scotland, which makes it very desirable that he should visit that country; and he has determined to start by the last of April or first of May.

The charge of the farm and homestead has been given to a trustworthy neighbour, who is to inhabit the house during his absence ; and Jessie and Willie are to accompany their cousin to her Western home, to recommence at a school the studies so long interrupted.

They cannot bear to leave the dear old farm that has been home to them all their lives. Willie wanders through the woods when "sugar-making" season begins, as if each maple-tree demanded a separate and special farewell; while it seemed to Jessie as if the last pleasant association of childhood was being taken from her.

It is well for her that there is much to be done in making preparations for their long absence; for the necessity of action alone could draw mind and memory from long "backward glances," almost fatal to her self-control.

This necessity is developing and strengthening that energy, without which any character—whether manly or womanly—is imperfect, and the loss of which renders the greater part of humanity comparatively useless.

April showers have washed away the last soiled remnants of snow, and fields of fall-wheat are beginning to look green and bright in the spring sunshine, before their preparations are all completed.

Mr Grey is to accompany them to Toronto, and see them settled in their new home before he proceeds upon his long journey; and they are to start away in less than a week. Willie has persuaded Jessie to go with him to the school-house, to say good-bye to the teacher and familiar class-mates he is leaving for strange ones far away.

It is early in the afternoon as they start upon the

walk they have so often taken together. Their hearts are full of the past, of memories of the little sister who used to be their companion, and of the sad day when she went from them for ever.

They come to the ridge, and Willie is hurrying past the spot, so strongly and painfully connected with his first great sorrow, when Jessie gently detains him, and they stand silently picturing to themselves the scene enacted there.

At first they look only at the water, so black and still in the shadow of the high bank, so strong and restless in its cruel depths, and have no thought of anything beyond. Willie is still sadly rehearsing the events of that October evening, when Jessie's voice calls him back to the present and brighter thoughts. " What a view of the grand old river we get from here ! I think the islands look better than from any other place ; and I mean to fix them in my mental picture-gallery, so that I may see them at will, though I am two hundred miles away ! " She speaks so cheerfully, almost gaily, that her brother does not dream of the effort by which, for his sake, that cheerfulness is assumed, as he raises his eyes to take in the whole breadth of the majestic river, and its varied beauties.

As he does so, there comes before him a vision of a bright summer morning, and a sweet, childish form standing beside him on this same elevation, looking with wistful earnestness at the lovely landscape, and he hears again the gentle tones of the voice saying, dreamily, "It makes me think of the ' pure river of the water of life ! '" Can he be sad when he believes that she is walking upon the banks of that crystal river ? Ought he to grieve that she has entered the home she so loved to think about when here ? Ah, no ! he will not wish her back ; but will be glad that she has escaped the evil, and will never feel the " chilling winds," of earthly sorrows !

Made hopeful by the thought of that land, and rejoicing that their treasure is there in the keeping of the same omniscient Father who is leading them, they resume their walk, sorrowing " not, even as others which have no hope."

They go quietly on, along the river shore, past the great " corner rock," and enter the woods, before either is ready to break the not unpleasant self-communing caused by the objects around them and their inseparable associations.

The opening buds of the trees are beginning to show a faint tinge of green, and " spring's first warblers " are already twittering from the gray branches, as they select the airy sites of their summer homes. And there, close to the trunk of a great old elm, Jessie spies a wee, modest flower, and stooping to gather it, finds that there are countless clusters beneath the light covering of last year's faded leaves! Every sorrowful thought is cast off for a time in the pure and entire pleasure of finding and admiring the tiny blossoms. A pleasure, simple as it is, that many an older and graver heart than theirs has equally shared, and been made forgetful by.

The first flowers of the spring-time! The old childish joyousness comes back as we search for the hidden tufts, as we brush away the leaves and twigs from their stems with all the old eagerness, and compare the delicate shades of blue and pink and violet, with all the old enthusiasm.

Ah! sweet May-flowers! your pure petals have beguiled many a heart-sick one to the fairyland of childhood, and brought forgetfulness of the many weary seasons that have come between its careless gaiety and the burden of to-day! Ye are ministering spirits, messengers of Him who "clothes the grass of the field," and are sent by Him to repeat to human hearts His lesson of faith—"Shall He not much more clothe you?"

But we must not leave our little friends too long, even in the pure companionship of the flowers; for the afternoon is wearing away, and the school-house is still to be reached.

There is more of the old brightness in Willie's face than has visited it for many long weeks; and a quiet gladness and lightness of spirit that have taken possession of his sister, show that the voiceless preachers have well fulfilled their mission.

They find school just dismissed, and stand upon the smooth rock before the door, while they exchange kindly greetings and farewells with the boys and girls with whom they are acquainted.

The hearty sympathy of their old friends, and the evident sorrow they feel at parting with them, bring back the painful sense of separation that is so hard to bear ; and when the last hand has been shaken, and the last caress received, they enter the school-house, feeling as if they were breaking off every tie that binds them to the old home and life.

The warm and affectionate reception they receive from Miss Mills is mingled with just enough of pity and sympathy to prove too much for Willie's already over-burdened heart ; and leaning his head upon his own old desk, while memory brings to mind all the sad changes since she was first his teacher, both past and present sorrows are expressed in an uncontrollable burst of tears.

After a few tender words, that show her appreciation and regard for his feelings, Miss Mills, judging that he will be able to quiet himself best if left alone, turns to Jessie. She is struggling hard to retain the outward composure that has become habitual to her ; but the tearful face that meets hers, and the gentle whisper, "I know what it is, dear Jessie ; my mother is dead, and I have left my own old home, never to see it again!" touch too nearly the quivering heart-strings, and with no thought or power of self-control, she throws herself into the arms so lovingly extended.

For a few moments their tears flow in an utter abandonment of sorrow, and Jessie's heart lightens itself for the first time, in the embrace of one who understands and entirely sympathises with her feelings.

Miss Mills is the first to regain composure, and in a little while her quiet tones, so full of confidence and heartfelt trust in the One of whom they speak, calm and soothe the weeping children, and bring back to their minds the glorious hope of reunion with the loved ones "gone before." She leads them insensibly from the sad thoughts of leaving their home to the pleasures and enjoyments of school-life—the many new friends they will find, and the new duties and obligations that will rest upon them. Many a word of kindly advice and direction is mingled with the cheerful surmises and fancies by which she accomplishes her purpose of lessening their grief at going away.

She accompanies them a part of the way home, and leaves them, at last, more hopeful for the future, and with kindlier thoughts of its changes, than they could have believed possible a few hours before. They have both promised to correspond with her, and she has engaged to keep them informed of all that goes on at the old farm and neighbourhood in their absence. " Write to me as freely as if I were a sister," she has said to Jessie, " and I promise to do all in my power to help and guide you. I am sure you will remember the one best Friend, whom alone we may depend upon at all times ; and depending upon Him, the world is powerless against us ! "

The gathering shades of evening warn them to quicken their steps, as they come out of the woods to the river-path ; and the end of their brisk walk finds them prepared to sit down to the waiting tea-table with brighter faces and more cheerful talk than has enlivened it for a long time.

Their wild-flowers are placed in a great soup-plate, the edges of which are covered with sprays of evergreen from the garden ; and the evident delight of the children in arranging and admiring their addition to the table attracts even Mr Grey from his usual gravity. Miss Mills was telling them of the wee English daisies of her old home, as they walked through the woods; and from them they go to their favourite wild-flowers—and *violets*, and *columbines*, and *honeysuckles*, and *maiden's-hair*, and a dozen others, are discussed with great animation. Mr Grey tells them of the Scottish gowan, of which he had often heard his father speak, and recites Burns's poem *To a Mountain Daisy* for them. They go to bed at last, having received in their hearts the sermon of the flowers—and having accepted the belief that the same Power that causes them to break forth from their wintry graves at the coming of the spring, will also quicken and bring to a glorious resurrection the bodies of those who sleep in Jesus, and will care, too, for them upon the earth, who put their trust in Him.

The few days that come between this and their last at home are quickly gone. They have visited and said good-bye to the graves in the lonely graveyard ; they have taken a farewell look at the old house ; and have grasped the last friendly hand of all but their own home-friends, the day before. And now, in the early morning, they meet together in the dear old room, so full of memories and associations, and bow for a parting blessing, to attend them in their wandering.

There are tearful eyes and aching hearts about the nice breakfast-table, at which appetites are sadly neglectful ; and then the carriage is at the door that is to convey them to the station.

Jessie runs up to her own little room, and there sinking upon her knees, repeats her mother's last prayer for her—" That she may be kept from the evil of the world ; and that God will be her guide through all the paths of life!" And then she comes down with a quiet face, to get through the last sorrowful leave-takings.

It is hardest of all to part from Grandma Bernard! She has known and loved them since their infancy, and they cannot hope to meet her again upon the earth. "May thy mother's God watch over you, my precious child! May He keep you 'unspotted from the world,' for the sake of His own Son!" is whispered by the faltering lips of the old woman, as she clasps Jessie in her arms.

She breaks away at last, and is seated by the side of her brother; to be quickly borne out of sight of the white walls of her home, and the watching group before the door. The familiar grounds are passed over, and all the well-known objects have disappeared. There is no interest for them in the strange houses and people upon the roadsides now; and they sit in perfect quiet until the station is reached. They are soon seated in the cars, to be swiftly carried away in the direction of their new home.

The novelty of their surroundings, and the many strange faces and scenes around them, quickly attract their minds from sorrowful remembrances; and by and by the going away does not seem such an absolute evil after all.

They are hurried on, past towns and across bridges,

through deep-cut passages in the rocks; and over high banks, from which they look down upon the surrounding country as upon a map spread at their feet.

Each and all of these varied scenes equally delight Willie, and afford subjects for unbounded wonder and satisfaction. He applies to his father for information on a great variety of questions, and becomes more impressed, with each answer, by the number of things he has yet to learn, and the necessity of study in order to understand the commonest things about us.

At *Kingston Mills* they take a last look at the St Lawrence—their "own old river, they will not see again for so long a time!" Willie exclaims sorrowfully. But his father points out the locks of the Rideau Canal, and describes its course, from the opposite window; and by the time it is talked over, the blue waters are lost sight of, and with them his momentary sadness.

Jessie's more thoughtful mind is not so easily made forgetful. Though sometimes diverted for a few moments by the conversation of her papa and brother or some passing object, it returns very often to the home she has left, and makes many an imaginary voyage into the opening future.

The memory of the prayers offered for her in that home gladdens her heart as she sits apparently interested in the scenery along the way; and unalloyed confidence in the One to whom they have been offered drives away all doubt and fearfulness. Her heart fixes itself upon a favourite verse of her mother's : "We know that all things work together for good to them that love God ;" and she rests in trustful faith, confident in her love for Him who "*first* loved us."

On dashes the tireless steam-engine through field and village, and wood and plain, bearing its heavily-freighted train of cars, in the pride of its matchless power ! On and away from their home, it carries Jessie and Willie Grey along the northern shore of blue Ontario, until, late in the afternoon, they enter the loyal old county, York.

They are all tired enough to welcome the first glimpse of the waters of the bay, and the houses and spires of the Queen City as they come in sight. Even Willie is quite satisfied to know that his day's journey is at an end, and ready to appreciate the cheerful hospitality that greets him in entering his new-found home in Toronto.

CHAPTER IX.

Life in the New Home.

" Early hath Life's solemn question
    Thrilled within thy heart of youth,
With a deep and strong beseeching—
    What and where is *Truth ?* "
             —WHITTIER.

BY the third week of May, Jessie and Willie have commenced their school-work in real earnest, and are beginning to feel quite at home in their new surroundings.

Mr Grey remained with them as long as it was possible, and left them at last, as far as his exertions could accomplish, provided with everything to make them contented and happy.

His eldest sister, Mrs Burns, with whom the children are to live during his absence, promises to be a kind and affectionate guardian to the loving niece and warm-hearted, impulsive nephew committed to her care.

They are already much attached to " Aunt Margaret," and all doubts of happiness in their new home are banished. They are, as yet, little acquainted with their uncle, his business detaining him from home a great part of the time ; and the cousin that was with them so long at the East is the only other member of the family.

They reside in one of the principal business localities of the city, and Jessie and Willie find a never-failing source of amusement in watching the throngs of people who pass and repass in the crowded street.

Comfortably established in the wide seat of an upper window, they look down upon the moving figures, study the strange faces, and speculate upon the business that calls them forth. Very often a glimpse of the sparkling waters of the bay, from between two lofty buildings, or beyond and above the roof of a humbler one, draws them from all recollection of the busy street. Sometimes thought flies from it to the great ocean, upon whose breast their dearest earthly friend is now being borne ; and sometimes to the St Lawrence waters, that roll so close to the old home shores ! They can see the sheen and gleaming of its waves in memory's faithful picture ;—each curve and island, each grove and field upon the shore, each far-away hill and hollow, fading away into dim, hazy outline upon the opposite bank ; and the hum of the noisy street comes to their ears

79

like the old murmur of the waves that wash the shores, the old rippling song they loved to listen to through all their childhood's years !

They sit together as the twilight deepens over the great city, as footsteps become fewer, and sound more distinct in the lessening bustle ; while memory brings before them the days gone by—the loved ones who are no more, and the light-hearted joyousness that the passing away of these seems to have taken from them for ever. But they turn to Him whose care is never removed ; they feel His presence with them still, and take courage for the coming days, sure that no evil can prevail against them while they trust in Him.

And thus a mother's prayers are answered, as her children repeat them in the quiet evening-time; for the ear of the Lord is ever open to the voice of supplication, and " they that wait upon Him shall renew their strength."

As the days pass on, school-duties press more heavily, and there are fewer moments that can be spared for watching the people in the street. The twilight, however, generally finds them at the window. Here they recount the day's experiences, and sympathise with one another in their respective trials or successes ; and here is kept strong and entire the bond that should be found in every brother's heart—the pure and perfect bond of a sister's love and sympathy !

Letters have been received from Mr Grey, announcing his safe arrival in Scotland, and describing his pleasure at finding himself amid the scenes of his father's early life, in the dear old home to which that father's heart had always so lovingly turned.

The account of his voyage awakens in Willie's mind an ardent wish to become acquainted with " the mystery of the sea." To Jessie is privately confided his intention of not only visiting Scotland, but also of becoming a great traveller and navigator, when once he has got through with his school-days.

Bright, ambitious boyhood! Many a hard blow and bitter disappointment must come before its confidence and hopefulness are altogether dispelled. Many a sober lesson of reality and experience must be learned before its rainbow-coloured fancies and wonderful possibilities are all relinquished.

Willie is naturally of a buoyant, sanguine disposition, and though his extravagant dreaming has been checked, in part, by the events of the last year ; there still remains enough of the old spirit to build many a fair air-castle, and paint many a brilliant picture of what shall be in future years.

It is well that a veil conceals that mystic land of the future ! It is well that coming events do *not* cast their shadows before ! God mercifully keeps His children in ignorance of what a day may bring forth.

If it were not so, childhood and youth would be robbed of their greatest blessing, and hope would find no real resting-place in any human heart. Ah! let the children keep their trust and faith in the brave actions they dream of as theirs! let them believe that every fanciful plan will be worked out in the far-away future years! For the bitter waters of experience will soon enough be reached, and the hand of time will tear down the fair structures built by the imagination of a child.

Jessie and Willie are well pleased with their respective teachers. It was thought best by her papa and auntie to place Jessie at a school where attendance would only be required a few hours of the day, as too much confinement might affect her already delicate health.

Her classmates at Madam R——'s soon learn to love the gentle, brown-eyed girl, who moves about so quietly in her deep mourning dress, and who is always so ready to assist and oblige; while Madam herself is charmed by the evident delight she takes in learning and correctly reciting her lessons.

It is too bad, but it must be acknowledged to be a fact, that a studious, thoughtful school-girl is something of a rarity in many other establishments than this. Why should it be so, girls? Why should you carelessly let slip the opportunity for securing that "good thing, education ?" With it and that " one thing needful," the blessing of God, your happiness and contentment are in your own keeping. No matter where circumstances may place you, enjoyment may be found, if only the key of knowledge be yours to open the gates of your surroundings.

Forest and plain, river and quarry, city and country, are alike full of eloquent teachings to those who are capable of understanding them. And thanks to our noble school-system, every Canadian girl may secure this capacity. *Be in earnest*, school-girls. Take home to your hearts the homely adage of your grandmothers, "Whatever is worth doing at all, is worth doing well." And by making it the motto of your school-life it will become the rule of all the after-time, until God says, " Well done."

Willie Grey finds himself in a very different position, at first, from that which he had occupied in the old Rock school-house at home. There, of late, and especially in the summer months, he had been one of the head boys of the school ; while here he finds himself among the youngest and least advanced pupils. Steady perseverance and industry, however, accomplish great things, and soon he is as much a favourite with teachers and classmates as ever in the far-away district-school. Toronto life, in reality, is a very different thing from the dismal, home-sick existence he had pictured while walking about the old farm two months ago ; and he enters heartily into the duties and enjoyments of the present, all the more heartily, perhaps, because of their contrast to what he had imagined about them.

The summer vacation soon begins. Mr Burns surprises and delights them by proposing that it shall be spent at Niagara Falls.

Willie is almost wild with joy when he first hears of the plan, and Jessie's pale face lights up with a very pleased expression as her aunt and cousin describe the nice, quiet farm-house at which they have twice before boarded through the hot summer months.

They tell her, laughingly, that her preference for the St Lawrence will all be gone when she has visited Niagara ; but she is quite sure that nothing can rival, or even be compared in beauty, with its well-known and well loved shores, and that not even Niagara's grandeur will make her declare against it.

" I hope you will like it well enough to get some colour from its breezes for these white cheeks," says her uncle ; " though, if you are ungrateful enough to be thinking of those eastern waters all the time you look at it, we can hardly expect it to forgive the slight to its superiority ! "

Jessie smilingly assures him that there is room in her heart for other scenes and other persons, though those of of the old home are remembered, and kept in the warmest place.

Mr Burns has taken a great fancy to his little niece, and it is principally upon her account that the visit to the Falls has been thought of and proposed.

He is to accompany them to their boarding-house, which has already been secured by letter, and then return to his business until the week before the re-opening of school.

They are to travel in their own conveyance, so that they may drive about the country at their pleasure during their long stay ; and Willie takes great pride in convincing his uncle that he is quite an accomplished driver and manager of horses.

School closes upon the 3rd of July, and the early morning of the 4th finds them in all the bustle and excitement of starting. The first faint dawn of light is stealing over the sleeping city as they drive through the last street and enter the open country, and by the time the sun's rays begin to grow uncomfortably warm, they have reached the little village in which they are to remain through the heat of the day. It is about midway between Toronto and Hamilton ; and another pleasant drive in the cool evening hours brings them to the last-named city.

In the afternoon of the next day, they arrive at Beechwood farm, which is to be their home for the two following months. Its owner is an old and valued friend of Mr Grey, and everything has been prepared that the kind-hearted farmer's wife could think of to add to the pleasure of his children.

Jessie and Willie are delighted when they find that their host and hostess have known their papa, and listen with unbounded pleasure to their reminiscences of long-ago days, in which his name very often occurs.

Leaving them thus pleasantly situated, Mr Burns returns to the city, having made Willie's heart glad by giving the carriage and horses into his care.

Then follow such delightful, care-free days! such walks, and drives and charming little picnics as are planned by Aunt Margaret! Oh! it is the very perfection of idle, pleasure-taking life! Jessie's cheeks are not ungrateful enough to withstand the combined influence of the free, pure air and abundant exercise, but regain the brightness lost so many months ago.

Letters come regularly from beyond the sea, so that there is no need of anxiety as far as their papa is concerned, and they hear from the dear old farm very frequently. There is nothing to prevent a thorough enjoyment of all the pleasures provided for them, and they have no intention of borrowing troubles for that purpose!

Beechwood farm is about three miles from the Falls, and their first visit is, of course, made there.

" It is no wonder," Jessie thinks, as she stands, looking at the mighty torrent, "that St John compared the voice of God to the noise of many waters." The terrible and solemn grandeur of the scene before her brings to her mind more forcibly than anything else has ever done the greatness and majesty of Him whose "spirit moved upon the face of the waters," whose word divided them, and "created the heavens and the earth ! "

She thinks, with grateful remembrance, that the same Spirit has visited her humble, child-like heart, that the same Voice has called her child. Even now, in the roar of the cataract, she hears Him whisper " It is I ; be not afraid."

Willie climbs from one point of observation to another, all eagerness and excitement, and is disappointed and half-impatient with his sister's few quiet words of admiration. "I didn't dream it was half so grand !" he exclaims. "Why, Jessie, how can you stand so quietly ?" and away he bounds to look through the spray from a lower spot.

Jessie's flushed cheeks and tearful eyes reveal a depth of feeling stronger by far than any loudly expressed admiration. Mrs Burns, seeing them, is quite satisfied with her niece's appreciation of the sublime picture. But she does not understand the feeling that causes her tears; she does not know that Jessie is looking upon it, not as a grand master-piece of nature, but as a new revelation of the majesty and power of Him who created it; of Him who humbled Himself and became obedient even to the death of the cross; of Him who "became a Man of sorrows and acquainted with grief" for the sins of the world; of Him who is now interceding for those for whom He died! Oh! she realises the greatness of the sacrifice that was offered for her, and consecrates herself anew to follow His footsteps in the "narrow way which leadeth unto life."

"From nature up to nature's God!" This should be the impulse of every Christian heart; and only when this direction is gained can nature be fully appreciated and enjoyed.

They come to the Falls very often during the summer, until almost every rock and shrub and form of spray is grown familiar; but in each visit, the first lesson repeats itself to Jessie's fancy, and the same feeling comes back as if she were standing very near the holy ground of God's presence!

Other favourite drives there are along the steep banks of the beautiful Niagara river. Many a time they follow its course as it surges down from the Falls, boils and tosses high its waves in the whirlpool, or more slowly and majestically descends towards the broad expanse of Lake Ontario. Sometimes the water itself far down the river near to the lake, where the current is scarcely felt, affords the means of passing a delightful day, when the hot summer sun makes even the woods too warm, and the cool, refreshing breeze, that seems to be a genius of the deep river-bed, is doubly grateful.

But with all these pleasures time keeps moving steadily on, and the last week of vacation comes, bringing Mr Burns to take them back to the city. He professes himself to be quite satisfied with the effect of country air upon their health, and expresses some fears that so long a time of idleness will make distasteful the return to study and work.

Hurried farewell visits are made to all the favourite resorts, and then their kind country friends are parted with, and the visit to Niagara is over.

They stay a day in Hamilton ; and the places of interest in and about this fine Canadian city are visited and admired by Jessie and Willie, with their uncle as guide, while their aunt and cousin are calling upon some friends and acquaintances.

The next day they reach Toronto, where, in spite of all the pleasure and idleness left behind, they welcome the sight of the familiar house and street, and each agree to the declaration of Mrs Burns, that it is good to be at home again, and she is glad to be there.

Willie settles himself next morning to write a long account of their vacation rambles for his papa, and

Jessie alternately assists his memory and her auntie, who is beginning to put in order the rooms of the house, that have been so long unused.

A letter is received from Miss Mills, telling them of the final sickness and death of Grandma Bernard. Many sorrowful recollections are awakened by the news, but their kind friend has so thoughtfully and skilfully reminded them of the release that their dear, old nurse has gained, and has mingled so many cheerful items in her sorrow-bearing pages, that they cannot encourage selfish sorrow with these before them.

"We have another friend in heaven, Willie, and that need not make us sad," says Jessie. "I am sure that is the way Miss Mills wants us to look at it; and the same love that took those who are gone from us will provide more when we need them."

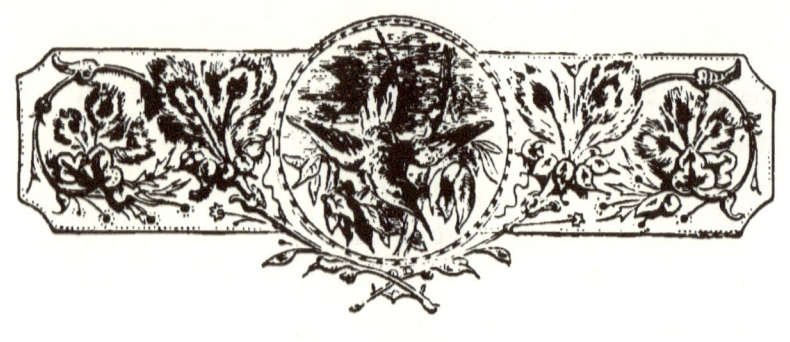

CHAPTER X.

A Word in Season.

" Follow with reverent steps the great example
Of Him whose holy work was 'doing good;'
So shall the wide earth seem our Father's temple,
Each loving life a psalm of gratitude."
—WHITTIER.

E have not time to follow Jessie and
Willie through all the varied experiences of school-life, and there is nothing
in theirs very unusual to the every-day trials
and pleasures of all students.

A difficulty arises the first week of the new
term, that, for a time, threatens to affect Willie's
enjoyment of the play-hours at school; but it
is soon overcome by the bold and resolute
manner in which he meets it.

A few of the boys who were in the same
classes with him when he first entered school,
were rough, and sometimes very profane in their

conversation. As they were naturally among the earliest with whom he became acquainted, he was obliged to listen to their talk and join in their games at first, but in a few days he withdrew himself from their society, and sought that of more congenial companions. They did not suspect the cause of his leaving them, and after a few good-natured attempts to recall him to their side of the play-ground had proved ineffectual, they left him to choose his own friends.

Willie was glad that he had been able to break off from such associates so easily, and did not dream of any further trouble arising from it.

His papa had warned him of the danger of "evil communications" in his last advice to him, and he often repeated it to himself as his first term at school passed away so pleasantly, and thought it was not very difficult to follow : "Be particularly careful, my boy, to guard against the temptations of *little sins.* Speak no word that you would not wish your sister or me to hear, and make no boy your friend who does. Keep from the first wrong step, and you will be kept from all." Poor Willie changes his mind about the difficulty of observing these directions when, at the beginning of the new term, he is called upon to test the strength of the principle that he professes to be guided by.

Some careless observation, made one day in the

presence of the worst of these boys, leads him to suspect Willie's motives for preferring other society than
theirs, and a few skilful questions soon satisfy him
that his suspicions are correct. At once begins that
system of persecution, hardest of all for a school-boy to
bear. Ridicule and sneers, hard names and cutting
jests, are, for a time, the weapons which meet and try
his patience and power of self-control, and though he
does not think of yielding, he cannot enjoy himself in
such surroundings.

Jessie tries to comfort and sustain him under the
trial, by assuring him that he is in the right, and that
even those who are most annoying must respect him in
their hearts.

"But you have no idea what it is like, Jessie, to have
the boys act so, and treat you as if they believed you
were the hypocrite and mean sneaking fellow they talk
about."

"I know it must be very hard, dear Willie ; but they
will soon be tired, when they see that you are not influ-
enced by their jeers, and they will grow ashamed of
such one-sided quarrelling. Keep a brave heart for a
little time longer, and you 'll completely conquer them."

A few more days of forbearance, and her words are
verified. The boys, finding that Willie is not to be
moved from his stand-point of right by all their raillery,
and feeling an inward consciousness that his side of the

question is by far most honourable, soon leave him to follow his own views, undisturbed by them.

And so this "shadow of mischance" passes away, having fulfilled its mission of showing Willie Grey his weakness and dependence upon a stronger Power, and leaving him strengthened for the greater conflicts yet to come in his battle with the world. And it is not without its influence among the other boys. An added respect is felt by those who share in his feelings, and even those who were bitterest against him, in their hearts honour the boy who is firm enough to "stand true to his colours," and the principle that upholds them.

September passes away, and October's frosts begin to paint the foliage with the gorgeous dyes that autumn produces in our Canadian climate. Amid many sad remembrances connected with this season, there come to Jessie and Willie memories of their old nutting-excursions, and visions of hickory and butternut trees, now dropping their fruit for other fingers to gather.

They comfort themselves as best they may for the loss of those pleasant days in the woods, by thinking of the more enduring enjoyment they are providing for themselves, in gathering the fruit of the tree of knowledge, a tree whose supply never fails, but is produced more abundantly as the demands upon it are increased.

Jessie is still applying herself to study as earnestly as at first, and every day finds her more delighted and interested. Vague ideas stand out clear and substantiated in the light of science and philosophy, and she tastes eagerly the drops of wisdom that the pages of her text-books furnish. She has learned to love some of the girls at school very dearly, and in general her days pass pleasantly and happily ; but sometimes a tiny cloud will shadow the brightness, and remind her of the transitory and unreliable nature of happiness which depends only upon earthly things.

She has not neglected to use the kind privilege Miss Mills allowed her of writing to her for advice and sympathy in all her troubles, and many a practical lesson has been learned from the few loving words by which her friend answers her appeals.

Perhaps we can best get an idea of these difficulties by reading a part of one of Jessie's letters, written a few weeks before the close of the Fall term :—

"I am afraid you will begin to tire of my long stories, but you have always helped me so readily, and cleared away all my doubts, that I feel as if I must come to you with everything. The questions that perplexed me seem so plain and simple after you have analyzed them, that I wonder they ever troubled me, or how I could have been at a loss in deciding about them.

"You know that school closes in a short time now, and some of the girls are to leave finally at Christmas.

Well, a few of us were sitting together the other day, talking of the holidays, and telling what we intended to do when we got through with school-life; and Nellie Bleecker, one of the girls who finishes at Christmas, told of all the grand parties and gay round of pleasure she expected to be engaged in, and the idle, care-free life she would begin then. Some of the girls said they envied her so much enjoyment, and wished they had nothing to do but looking for amusement for themselves. I suppose I looked grave, for one of them said, 'I imagine you think it is sinful to waste time in such things, don't you, Jessie?' They all looked at me, and Nellie repeated the question with a careless laugh. I scarcely knew how to answer for a moment; but they seemed to expect a reply, so I said that I thought there was something for us each to do, and that God required more from us than the mere seeking of our own pleasure.

"'But don't He want us to be happy and enjoy ourselves?' said Nellie; 'what was life given us for, if not to be enjoyed?' All the girls agreed that they believed as she did, and declared that there was nothing else to live for, if that object were taken away.

"I thought of my mother's life, and of many others that I know were far happier than they could have been if they had lived only for their own enjoyment; and then that one sentence, which some one has said

96

contains the whole history of Christ's life upon earth, came into my mind, '*He went about doing good.*' I tried to express my ideas to the girls. I said that God wanted us to be happy, but that the only real happiness was found in trying to work for Him, and in knowing that our happiness for the life eternal was secured. I thought of all He bore and suffered for us, and how little He esteemed His own comfort through all the weariness and pain of His sojourn upon earth, and remembered that those who follow Him alone make the best use of life. Perhaps I spoke too earnestly, or the girls misunderstood me, for no one said a word when I stopped talking, and some of them have scarcely spoken to me at all since. I am very sorry. I would not like them to think that I set myself up as better than they, or that I tried to teach them. And yet I do not feel as if I said more than I could help, since they asked me. Tell me if I am wrong, and what I should do to make my part right."

The same day that the letter containing these passages was posted, Jessie finds that she need not have been troubled about the effect of her earnest words, as far, at least, as one of her hearers is concerned. Nellie Bleecker, the young lady mentioned in Jessie's letter, is the daughter of a wealthy and fashionable gentleman in one of the western counties. Left motherless at a very early age, her life has been spent at boarding-schools, and among gay and thoughtless relations. Her beauty and accomplishments, added to a very charming manner, have made her a favourite at Madam R——'s ; and Jessie was very much grieved when their pleasant intercourse seemed likely to be discontinued.

Miss Bleecker's boarding-house is but a short distance from Mr Burns's residence, and she generally calls for Jessie on her way to school. For the last few days, however, she has seemed to avoid meeting her, and Jessie has had no opportunity for asking an explanation of what is giving her so much pain.

She is very glad, therefore, to find Nellie waiting for her again as she is starting to school this morning, about a week after the conversation which we have read in the letter to Miss Mills.

They greet one another affectionately, and Jessie says, gently, "Then you forgive me, Nellie, for unintentionally offending you, the other day ?"

"*Forgive* you ! Oh, Jessie ! I cannot forgive myself for the sinful waste of time your words showed me my eighteen years of life has been. I want you to teach me more ; show me how to make amends for the past !"

Tears are falling fast from Jessie's eyes, and Nellie's mind is too disturbed and anxious to become interested in the lessons that await her at school, so she proposes that they get excused from the morning's recitations, and go back to her room, where they can talk undisturbed.

"I have been so unhappy and dissatisfied with my-self, through all this week!" she says. "I tried to drive your words away by thinking of the gay life I have looked forward to so long; but the thought of that eternal life you spoke of came between all my bright fancies, and shadowed all my pictures. And your patient, sorrowful face has been preaching to me every day, until, this morning, I resolved that 1 would come to you, and ask you how I must begin to live in earnest."

"I can only point you to the example which has been given to us all," says Jessie. "'To love God and keep His commandments,' Jesus said, is life eternal. We can do nothing more."

"But I do not know how to come to Him. I am afraid I do not love Him as I ought, and I do not know how to begin."

"His own Word will teach you that, dear Nellie. It is impossible to read of all that He has done and suffered for us, and not love Him; and loving Him, we must obey and follow Him."

"But it seems so strange, Jessie, that the enjoyment of the world must be given up, and all our amusements and pleasures! I cannot understand that."

"And God does not require us to relinquish them, Nellie. It would not make you enjoy to-day's pleasure less, would it, if you knew that the happiness of the next *year* were secured? And in the same way the children of God may enjoy the pleasures of this life, even while looking forward to the assured happiness of the life beyond. One who is really His child," she continues, "and who tries most to be like Him and follow Him, will not take pleasure, or spend his life in frivolous amusements ; but will try to fulfil the solemn duty that rests upon him, of teaching others the knowledge he has gained."

Long and earnestly the girls talk together; Jessie, with her simple, child-like faith, being, perhaps, a better teacher for Nellie's newly-awakened anxiety than any learned theorist could have been. She tells of the sorrowful passages in her life that have taught her, most of all, to cling to the one immovable support ; and Nellie realizes in part what that faith must be which has enabled the gentle, timid girl beside her to " suffer and be strong."

"I believe I see a glimmering ray of the light that is so plain and bright to you, dear Jessie," she says, at last ; "and I will search and pray until it shines upon me, too, in its full radiance !"

They part from one another at last, each feeling a new interest and tenderness springing up in her heart, and having become better friends, through the conversation of these few hours, than all the previous months of school-intercourse had made them.

The friendship commenced this bright December day strengthens and increases in after-years; and many times, when school-days are long past, they meet and talk over the influences and events of the morning that first broke through the reserve of mere acquaintance, and made them life-long friends.

And Jessie Grey goes on rejoicing, in the quiet path through which the present leads her; but as she "keeps the noiseless tenor of her way," she does not forget the words of the wise man, but often experiences for herself that " a word fitly spoken is like apples of gold in pictures of silver."

CHAPTER XI.

"And the Years glide by."

"I sit by the hearth of my early days;
All the home-faces are met by the blaze,
And the eyes of the mother shine soft, yet say,
It is but a dream: it will melt away!"
—Mrs Hemans.

THE winter passes away very quietly and uneventfully to our student friends in Toronto.

Mr Grey has been, for some months, uncertain as to the time of his return to Canada, but, with the opening of the spring, a letter is received expressing his intention of remaining in Scotland at least another year. He has entered into some business relations that promise to pay well; and being quite satisfied that the farm at home is in good hands, he has decided to stay until Jessie has quite finished the course of study she has commenced.

Mr and Mrs Burns are glad to keep her with them as long as possible, and even Jessie, though longing to see her papa again, is not sorry to have her time at school thus lengthened.

Though not without many both pleasant and unpleasant incidents, the succeeding year and a half of her stay in Toronto brings nothing very remarkable, and makes but little change in the gentle, womanly nature we have known so long. A deeper knowledge of the world and its varieties of character is gained; but the trusting faith of earlier years is still in her heart, and a stronger dependence upon Him who has guarded her so long daily answers her mother's dying prayer, and keeps her yet " unspotted from the world."

Willie's summer vacation is spent at his dear St Lawrence home, and such glowing accounts of its pleasures and enjoyments are given in his letters to Jessie, that she half regrets being persuaded to forego them for any others. She accepted the urgent invitation of her friend, Nellie Bleecker, to spend a part of the holidays with her, and very happy days those of her visit prove themselves. Nellie is housekeeper for her papa in their luxurious western home, and Jessie receives such a joyous welcome, and is so overwhelmed by loving attentions, that Willie's letters lose all their power of causing regret. They live in a lovely spot upon the shore of Lake Huron, and everything that

refined taste and abundant means could suggest or
supply has been done to increase the natural beauty of
their surroundings. Delightful drives, boating excur-
sions upon the lake, long evening walks, and pleasant
morning rides, succeed one another through the weeks of
Jessie's stay; and the two girls enter into all these pleasures with all the zest and earnestness of girlish interest
in "something new." They find time, too, for many
long, quiet talks—talks in which they forget the gaiety
of the present, and discuss soberly and seriously the
great life-question of every human heart; that old,
often-answered question, "*What is Life ?*" that has
puzzled many older and wiser ones than they, and
which, alas! so many fail entirely in answering aright.
But they have been taught its meaning through the
unerring counsel of God's Word, and have, in their
simple, reverent faith "sat at His feet" to learn, and
be prepared for its fulfilment. How much beyond that
wisdom which, through wearisome study and toil, has
endeavoured to penetrate and comprehend the mystery
of Him who was *God* and *man*, is the unquestioning
confidence of those "little ones" by whom His praise
is "perfected," for it is written, "Whosoever shall not
receive the kingdom of God as a little child, shall in
no wise enter therein!"

Jessie's visit comes to an end, as the pleasant things
of this life will do, and she returns to Toronto to begin

her last year at school. It is soon gone, and then the last farewell is given to teachers and classmates, and our little friend's student-life is over. She is now nearly eighteen, and bears away the honours of the school as "first graduate of the season," and, better than all else, she has secured and leaves behind her "loving favour and a good name," those precious things "rather to be chosen than great riches."

She says good-bye to the kind uncle and auntie who have so long been tender and careful guardians to her, and leaves the pleasant home they have provided, sorrowfully, and with reluctant feet.

But all sorrow for the friends left behind, and every feeling of reluctance, vanish as she approaches the dear old home she left so sadly nearly three years before. Other places may have beauties and attractions, but this is, after all, nearest her heart, and must ever be best loved.

She walks about the old familiar grounds, and through the silent house, with a "joy that is almost pain" in its very intensity.

But not much time can be given to musing. Her papa is expected the first week of September, and the three intervening weeks must be very busy ones, in order that everything may be prepared for his coming, and the old time look of cheerful comfort be given to the rooms and furniture. An efficient helper presents herself in the person of Miss Mills, no longer the district-school teacher, but the happy wife of the young minister, who has taken the place left vacant by the death of the old pastor. With her assistance, everything is arranged as it was in the days of the happy past, and each room appears as memory has pictured it to the wanderer in lands beyond the sea!

And then Jessie waits for his coming, while thought, stirred up by the sight of old associations and surroundings, makes many a visit to the shadowy land of the past.

> "Henceforward, listen as we will,
> The voices of that hearth are still;
> Look where we may, the wide earth o'er,
> Those lighted faces smile no more.
> We tread the paths their feet have worn,
> We sit beneath their orchard-trees,
> We hear, like them, the hum of bees
> And rustle of the bladed corn;
> But in the sun they cast no shade,
> No voice is heard, no sign is made,
> No step is on the conscious floor!"

All this comes home to the heart of the lonely girl; but there comes, too, the "hours of faith," that have taught her; that are still repeating, in loving tones—

> "The truth to flesh and sense unknown,
> That life is ever lord of death,
> And love can never lose its own!"

At last the trusty ship lands her "homeward bound"

passengers at Montreal, and Mr Grey is again upon his native soil, and breathing the pure Canadian air. The following day brings him to Jessie, and the very "home, sweet home," his heart has so yearned to see, is his once more. She is more than repaid for all her labour by the few words of thanks and blessing her father whispers as he enters it, and she goes to sleep that night as happily and peacefully as ever in her childhood ; while the murmuring of the waves upon the shore brings back the old joyous dreams, and repeats to her ears the old song she loved in the long ago.

Mr Grey was accompanied by one of the partners in the business of whose firm he had become a member, a half-cousin of his own ; and as there are many things to be looked after by him, and many visits to be made to old friends and neighbours, the duty of entertaining the young Scotchman devolves almost entirely upon Jessie. She is apparently very successful in removing prejudices, and exciting an admiration for her native land ; for when, some months afterwards, he goes back to the " Land of brown heath and shaggy wood," it is only to make preparations for a final return to Canada.

Willie is still in Toronto, entered now upon his course at the University, and carrying with him there the same strength of principle and energy that distinguished his boyhood. His father's most cherished wish is gratified by his decision to enter the ministry at the close of his college course ; and Jessie, too, is proud and happy in his choice. To her has been confided all his fears and doubts upon the subject, and she is glad to know that the voice of ambition and worldly gain has yielded to that of Him who still appoints them He has chosen and set apart for His special work.

Time forbids a longer history of the inmates of the white-walled farmhouse.   It still stands in its quiet atmosphere of peace and comfort, upon the sunny shore of the St Lawrence ; and it is probable that it will be Jessie Grey's home through all the days of her life upon earth.   We may leave her, with no fear for her future, secure in the love that is "never weary."   All that He sends or suffers to be will be accepted "as from the Lord," and faith will still see, beneath the seeming ill, the mercy and wisdom of Him who cannot err.

We would willingly linger about the dear old farm, and recount the events of the next few years.   How a church is erected upon the Point, upon the very site of the old loghouse where Mr Grey was born, and where we listened to the stories of Grandma Bernard upon that Saturday afternoon so long ago.   How a new school-house is built in the shade of the maple-trees beneath which we sat to eat our dinners upon our first

visit. How Willie makes great progress in his higher
studies, and writes home during the long college terms
letters full of interest to the various members of the
home circle, telling of achievements in arts, and in
arms as well, for he is learning to handle the rifle as a
member of the college corps, and how all rejoice that
his soldiering in earnest is to be in a better army.

And, if to-day we visited the old place, we would
listen again to the ringing of childish voices, and hear
the familiar names of Willie and Allie sounding through
the pleasant house.

It is but a few weeks since the Willie we have
known—the Rev. William Grey to strangers and the
world—came from his distant field of labour to look
again upon his childhood's home, and greet within its
walls the father and sister to whose loving advice and
sympathy he owes so much of the present good. Many
a long afternoon of his visit he spent upon the water,
sailing about among the islands he roamed over so
joyously as a boy, and recalling to mind many sweet
memories of the golden-haired child—his angel-sister
now. And the heart of the strong man rises in fervent
prayer, that, in all the paths of life, he may possess the
humble, trusting faith that found her so early prepared
to "depart and be with Christ," and that the same
power that has led them through the past will still

provide for whatever the future may bring, until they are united about His throne, to part no more for ever.

And so our story ends, having followed the life-paths of Jessie and Willie Grey up to this very year of 1869, having shown that the bitterest sorrows, when rightly interpreted by faith, prove to be a source of blessing, and that, "to them that love God, all things work together for good."

God grant, my child, whoever you may be, that your heart is prepared and strengthened by this love to accept the chastening He sends! God grant that if to you is given "great tribulation" in the present world, you may have washed your robes and made them white in the blood of the Lamb," and be thus fitted to be "before the throne of God, and serve Him day and night in His temple!"

No matter how successful your life may be to the eyes of the world, no matter how famous or wealthy your exertions in it have made you, if you have not trusted to the efficacy of the pardon bought by the blood of Christ, if you have not followed His footsteps and obeyed His laws, it can be but an entire failure, and will merit the dreadful sentence that was pronounced upon the faithless servant by Him who will be your judge!

Consider well and earnestly this one great question,

upon which depends, not only the real enjoyment of the world, but also the happiness or misery of *eternity.*

Upon one side there is *nothing*, upon the other rests *all.* Accept Christ, and you have a friend provided for every time of need; One who remains true when wealth and fame, and the dearest earthly relationships, are lost and broken ; One upon whom you may but lean more heavily in the darkest hour ; One who will " never forsake " them who trust in Him for strength. Reject the offers of His love, and you will remain all through life dissatisfied with your pleasures, with yourself, and the world. You will ever feel in your heart the restless *want* of a higher and more enduring source of enjoyment, and while you are seeking it, time will be drifting you away from the open gates of mercy to those of justice and retribution ! " Choose ye this day whom ye will serve," and let your choice be Christ ! "Remember now thy Creator in the days of thy youth, while the evil days come not, nor the years draw nigh, when thou shalt say I have no pleasure in them," for each of these years will remove farther the forgetful heart, and make more difficult its return.

Christ has died for *you.* Make now His love and His redemption personal to you, by accepting His own conditions, and consecrating to their fulfilment the life that He has given.

"AND THE YEARS GLIDE BY."

And when this life is over, when we are made immortal, and eternity begins, may our lamps be found burning, may we enter together the portals of our Father's glorious home, to go out no more for ever!

THE END.

PRINTED BY BALLANTYNE AND COMPANY
EDINBURGH AND LONDON

www.ingramcontent.com/pod-product-compliance
Lightning Source LLC
Chambersburg PA
CBHW020410030726
47496CB00007B/2396